ALEX LIDELL

LAST CHANCE ACADEMY

IMMORTALS OF TALONSWOOD

TILDOR

THE CADET OF TILDOR

SIGN UP FOR NEW RELEASE NOTIFICATIONS at https://links.alexlidell.com/News

1

―――――――――

Sam

*S*inking into the red vinyl booth at the back of the Lone Moon diner, I slide the manila envelope across the table. The paper whispers over coffee-stained plastic until the man on the other side pins it down with his fingers, as if trapping a mouse. His square jaw clenches as he scans my face, his golden eyes seeming capable of piercing skin. Then, with a flick of his fingers too fast to catch, he picks up the envelope. With his sleeves rolled up at the elbows, I can see the muscles of his forearms shifting as he pulls out the three photos inside, face as hard and unreadable as stone.

Breathe, Sam. I've never been intimidated by a client before, and I won't start now.

Why someone would want photos of a hundred-year-old deed from a lawyer's office, I have no idea. And I don't care. My clients don't come to me for questions. Given that the diamond signet ring on the man's finger is worth more than the Lone Moon itself, I assume he has his reasons for not just buying a copy.

Either that, or he's simply stupid. Considering he's wearing diamonds and a four-thousand-dollar suit to the Newark slums, odds are the latter.

Perhaps it's all a part of some cosmic fairness plan, the universe having to take something from the man to balance out that devastatingly beautiful face of his, with its chiseled angles and lashes so long, they belong on a Disney princess. Except on him, they look right. Just like his white-blond hair, tied back in a low knot. Everything on him looks right, from his strange eyes to the honed muscles sculpting his black silk shirt.

"Good morning, Samantha!" a waitress slides up to our table with her pot of house coffee—a day-old brew reserved for those who aren't paying five bucks for the handcrafted beverage choices— and sloshes some into my stained mug. "All topped off. Will we be having anything else today?" She flashes my companion a hopeful smile.

"Privacy," he says without bothering to look up. It's the first time I've heard him speak, and his soft Scottish burr nearly makes me jump.

The waitress's face tightens as she slaps the pot down on our table, striding away with a huff. In my head, I reduce my dinner money allowance to absorb the bigger tip I'll be leaving. The Lone Moon is a hard enough shift to work without having to put up with self-absorbed men.

I tap my fingers against the table while my client thumbs through the three eight-by-ten images. He shoots my fingers a swift, nearly imperceptible glance, and I stop abruptly, reminding myself to breathe.

It seems stealing these was the easy part—delivering them is turning out to be another thing entirely. The power seeping off my client is burning all the air in this stuffy diner, and not just for me. In every corner of the room, eyes, faces, and sometimes whole bodies turn in our direction, taking in the tall, leanly muscled man in slick black Armani.

I'm almost glad he arranged all this through a secretary now— that face is a distraction that no thief needs on the job.

I pull out my phone for something else to do with my hands. One missed text message, from Janie. A quasi-foster sister of mine, except that she's twelve and still in the system.

Court denied the stipend request.

I swallow a curse. Jamie is staying with Mrs. Leonards now, who isn't a bad sort, but she can't afford to support a twelve-year-old on what the state gives her. Another year and a fake ID, and Janie will be able to get a part-time job to help pay her upkeep. We just need Mrs. Leonards to hang on until then. Janie is a good kid. Too good for the system.

Tell Leonards I'll pay the stipend myself, I type back. *And don't let her rent the spare room out to Joey.*

A pause. Too long.

I type another message. *Janie?*

Leonards knows you can't even pay your own rent. It's all right. I'll manage.

"This is incomplete." The man's low voice pulls me back to the diner with a jolt, and I slip the phone back into my pocket without answering Janie. He jerks his chin at the photos. "The signature line is missing."

There we go with that high intellect. "A lot more than the signature is missing. Or, rather, missing from the envelope I just gave you."

He cocks his head, looking genuinely surprised for a brief moment, before his eyes flatten into implacable stones. My heart speeds up in spite of myself. This is a dangerous game I'm playing. But I have no choice.

"I photographed the whole file. This," I jerk my chin toward the photos, "is proof of life. Once you pay, you get the thumb drive with everything."

The man raises one pale brow, still giving nothing away. It's strange how his age is difficult to place—he seems in his midtwenties, only a few years older than me, but the aura of strength he carries feels much older. As if he truly owns the power young men usually only play at, cubs imagining themselves kings. Not him, though. He is for real. And that, more than anything, is setting me on edge.

Men with power never hesitate to use it. Just ask any other *graduate* of the New Jersey foster system—we all have scars to prove its true.

I cock a brow right back at him, staring him in the eye as if we were equals, as if we occupy the same plane of existence. I can fake power with the best of them.

He snorts. "You imagine I'd go through the trouble of cheating you out of *three hundred* dollars?"

Three hundred dollars might not be worth the bother to my new diamond-encrusted friend here, but for me, it's the ticket to getting my heat turned back on. "I am not *imagining* it one way or another. I'm just ensuring it doesn't happen."

Reaching into his pocket, the idiot pulls out a roll of hundred dollar bills right in the middle of the Lone Moon and counts off three Franklins, while I move the coffee pitcher to create a visual barrier.

The man's eyes flicker toward the pitcher, a tug at the corner of his mouth saying he understood exactly what I just did. That maybe he'd pulled the wad out just to make me squirm.

"There you go." Leaning in as he pushes the money toward me, he quirks his full lips into what could almost be called a smile—if the condescension dripping off him weren't quite so palpable. He truly is too beautiful for fairness, and his cologne—a woodsy musk with a splash of winter breeze—is enough to make my head spin. Or maybe that's my lack of breakfast today. Which is another correction that three hundred dollars will make.

"There you go." I slide the thumb drive across the table as I pocket my payment. Maybe three hundred will buy Janie another month. We'll see. Nodding to my client, I pick up the coffee bill.

The man pins the bill to the tabletop, our fingertips brushing for an instant that sends a zing of sensation through me.

"On me," he says with another dismissive half smile that makes my blood boil.

I yank back the check. "I pay my own bills, thank you."

Something shifts in his gaze that makes me go cold, suddenly all the condescension and half smiles seeming like a façade for something much deeper—and much more dangerous. "I insist," he says. It's so low, so commanding, that I pull back and lift my hands before I can stop myself. Then lower them, embarrassed—and furious with myself for reacting to his power grab like a scared little girl.

Right. That's enough of this asshole—and the effect he's having on me. I press both my palms into the tabletop, which lets me have some height on him. "I don't care for men insisting on anything. We aren't friends. We aren't acquaintances. We don't even have business together anymore. Now let me have my bloody bill and goodbye."

The man lifts his hand with dramatized slowness, showing me empty palms. "All yours. My name is Ellis, by the way, if you were wondering."

"I wasn't." I was. But I shouldn't have been. It's unprofessional and it's dangerous, giving people an illusion of camaraderie that we don't have. "Excuse me."

I slide out of the booth and start toward the register, only to realize Ellis is following me. Which is no longer funny, no matter how good-looking he is. I spin on him with a curse on my lips, which dies as quickly as it came. Standing, his presence and sheer size are impossible to ignore. He's even taller than I thought, standing at least a foot over my head. He casts a literal fucking shadow over me. I can feel his heat even from two feet away, sense the grace and restrained violence in every muscle of his body. Somewhat disguised in the booth, they seem to shimmer off him now, making other diners turn to look at him with full, open curiosity. Some with admiration, even lust in their eyes. Some with fear.

I know where I fall on that spectrum. My heart quickens, my muscles tightening to alert.

Scanning the tables, I spot a booth one row down, where a middle-aged couple has just finished eating, a steak knife now lying across one empty plate. Good enough. Plastering a huge, sparkling smile on my face, I walk down the row of tables and grab the dirty dish off the table.

"Let me get this out of your way," I tell the couple, walking on before they can ask for the dessert menu or whatever it is people who eat in restaurants do at this point.

"Message received." Ellis's Scottish-tinted words are soft behind me. "I come too close and ye stab me. Is there anything I've actually done to warrant this distrust?"

I snort. The whole question is a fallacy—distrust doesn't need to be earned; trust does. It's guilty until proven innocent in my world. Not that it matters since I don't pair up with anyone anyway. Hand around the knife hilt, I head to the register.

"The only problem is that this wee setup makes it verra difficult for me to try and hire you for another job," Ellis murmurs.

"No," I say without turning my head.

"Ten thousand dollars."

I stumble, the dish teetering in my hand before Ellis steadies it to prevent a fall, his warm fingers overlapping mine. When I look up at him, his golden eyes flash with real amusement for a moment as he hands the dish—knife and all—back to me. Just as quickly, he's back to cool indifference, and I wonder if I imagined it.

"Oh, I'll take that for you, hon." A new waitress appears, tugging on the plate. The sudden return to the normal world is as jarring as the sum Ellis just mentioned. Around us, the diner continues as normal, with the low buzz of conversation and the clatter of silverware against plastic platters. The waitress finally manages to liberate the plate from my grip. "Is there anything else I can get you?"

I blink, smiling to buy my racing brain more time to think. Ten thousand dollars. Holy blessed crap.

"An espresso for me, if you please," Ellis tells the waitress with a charming white grin, the woman's face turning a bright flustered pink. The guy's a chameleon—or just a full-on psycho. "Steak and eggs for the girl. Medium rare with a side of hash browns. Also a cappuccino. And orange juice."

"That's—" That's a twenty-dollar bill for breakfast. My head clears at once. *That's* why it never pays to spend too much time with any one person. "That's not what I want right now," I tell Ellis.

His eyes pin mine, making my chest tighten painfully. "I dinna care," he says. And there is nothing soft about his tone now.

2

Sam

The back of my mind warns that letting Ellis buy me breakfast will come back to bite me, that no matter what I told myself, I stuck around to listen as much for his golden eyes as for the business. Which I turned down. Ten thousand dollars or no, the request was too dangerous.

"Don't you break into houses all the time?" Janie asks when I pick her up from school so I can have a chat with Mrs. Leonards before the lady makes her decisions. "How is an empty mansion any different?"

"Alarm systems. Item value. A neighborhood where the police will actually show up to investigate." I nudge Janie to my other side as we pass a row of bail bonds businesses. We have three right next to each other on Main Street, all doing a booming business. We step automatically off the curb to go around a man speaking loudly to himself about the upcoming alien invasion, and I tug my wool cap lower over my ears, my leather jacket luckily taking the brunt of the autumn wind. "Plus, I don't trust Ellis. I don't want to work with him."

"You don't trust anybody," says Janie with a meaningful tilt to one brow. She's about ten years younger than I am, but sounds like an adult. With a slim, serious face, a long sheaf of dark brown hair, and the style sense of a high school librarian, she kind of looks like one too. Not that her second- and thirdhand clothing options leave her much choice. "Is that sustainable in the long term?"

I snort. "It's the only way to have a long term. You'll see."

"Is it bad that I trust you, then?" she asks.

I peer down at her, considering the question. "Well, I'm not a man, so that helps. But—" I stop short as we turn onto the residential block where Mrs. Leonards lives and spot the old Pontiac her stepson, Joey, drives. A moment later, the man himself appears, carrying boxes into the house.

My blood chills. Joey was the first man I had sex with. And it wasn't by choice. Just looking at the jiggling potbelly sends bile rising up my throat.

"It's all right." Janie makes herself sound sunny, though I can feel the strain. "I've met him before. He won't do anything—I don't think I'm his type."

Janie is female and twelve. She is exactly Joey's type. I quicken my step down the row of two-story apartments in various shades of brick and gray, and across the small yard in front of Mrs. Leonards's apartment, stepping around a collapsed beach chair. She's on the front porch by the time I get to the steps, that sugar-sweet smile on her plump, fatigue-lined face. "Samantha, dear, it is so good to see you again. How are you holding up? Have you gone to see any talent agents like I told you to? With that soprano voice of yours—"

"You can't let him live in the same house as Janie," I say, my heart beating hard as Joey changes course to come over to us. The tip of his tongue darts out, licking his thick lips. He looks like a sex offender out of central casting—stout and towheaded, a black death-metal T-shirt stretching over his barrel chest, pale skin running to blotchy, a badly trimmed mustache clinching the deal. I swallow, angling my body between him and the girl, relieved when I hear him walk past us into the house. "He's on the offender registry, Mrs. Leonards. He can't live in the same house as a foster child."

"Now, Samantha." Leonards's tone turns cool. "We all know Joey doesn't belong on that list. I need my son by my side. If Janie doesn't feel comfortable with the arrangement, however…" Pulling out her phone, Leonards hovers her finger over the keypad, her aged hand shaking slightly. She doesn't like Joey any more than I do, but the asshole is holding a whole box of food right now.

Janie's small hand covers the phone. "I'm fine with Joey, Mrs. Leonards," she says, throwing me a meaningful glance. "I'd rather stay here with you both than go to a different foster."

I grab Janie's arm. I have no heat at my place, or I'd take her there. Hell, I might not even have a place in a few months. Still. "Janie…"

She shakes her head, face pale but stubborn as rocks. "I'm not a child, Sam. I can do math. And I can take care of myself too."

Mrs. Leonards turns her face, but I catch the glistening tears pooling there. And the bruise. She has no more choice than any of us. Money is money.

"Give me two days," I tell them both, then turn into the wind.

"Samantha, don't," Janie calls, but now it's my turn to shake my head. I can take care of myself too, and the risk-reward ratio just shifted. Before I can change my mind, I pull out my phone and dial Ellis's number.

TEN THOUSAND DOLLARS TO retrieve an heirloom jewelry box from an empty mansion. One night's work. Plenty of reward for the risk. That's what I keep telling myself as I ignore the towering ivy-covered stone monstrosity above me and slide my knife along the windowpane, the thin blade guiding me right to the lock.

As usual, I don't pause to question why this comes so easily to me—why picking locks, hiding from pursuers, confusing security guards, and charming German shepherds all feel about as natural as breathing—and I especially don't pause to feel guilty about it.

A piercing howl suddenly shatters the night's silence, making me fumble my tools. I suppress a loud curse, pausing to let my heartbeat slow back down. This enclave is forested, sure, but it's still on the lush green outskirts of Upper Montclair, New Jersey's richest zip code, and the nearest houses are only a quarter mile away. Not wolf country. But who knows with these disgustingly rich types—the idiot owner probably bought and settled them here for his own entertainment.

My breath mists before my face in the chill, the puffs still coming steadily despite my slowly rising pulse. Closing my eyes, I move the tip of the blade inside the locking mechanism until the *click* of a spring giving way echoes softly in welcome. Sheathing the knife in my boot, I gently remove the windowpane, pausing for a moment just in case I'm wrong. In case the window is alarmed after all.

Not that the elite would ever bother to ask the thieves, but if I owned a mansion like this, set deep within a cul de sac well off the main roads, I'd have twenty-four seven armed security, let alone an alarm system. A private system, which would lead to some private company and not the police. Then again, maybe if I lived in a place like this, the police would give a damn about me.

Setting the windowpane on the ground beside the wall, I pull myself over the sill and into the silent house—and suppress a gasp. Even in the dark, it's astonishing. Ceilings so high, they disappear into the dark, four walls entirely lined with books. The moonlight glints off what look like huge stained-glass Tiffany lamps on each side table, just waiting to be plucked on by a lucky reader.

Even though I watched the place for the entire day just to make sure it was as empty as Ellis claimed, being here still gives me the chills. A counterbalance to the heat his memory sends through me, no matter how much I try to ignore it. Men like Ellis—men who are gorgeous and powerful and know it—are a little too used to getting their way. By any means necessary.

I think of Joey and remind myself that, actually, good looks are not even necessary.

Concentrate, Sam. Pulling my attention back to the quiet mansion, I note the slowly blinking red lights. So there *is* an alarm—just a poorly installed one. So long as I don't cross the line between the two sensors, I'll be fine.

This isn't my typical gig. Clients who can afford such homes can afford lawyers and private investigators and personal shoppers. Those who come to me to liberate items of interest aren't the ones who can afford to work inside the law—usually desperate souls who pawned away some heirloom and need it back, or need to get their stuff back from an ex who is too quick with his fists. Last week, I stole a back a little pit bull puppy, cuddling him inside my leather jacket as I got myself the hell out of the cesspool he was going to grow up in.

Dark dank places that the police wouldn't go near even if the whole neighborhood sent up a flare with directions. Newark's underbelly, that I can handle. The boys in blue, on the other hand—well, meeting with Newark's finest never ends well for a foster system brat who just can't appreciate her second chance properly. Even though I aged out of it a few years back, the memories are branded on me. Memories of what really happens to those who have no money to speak for them.

Literally. Opening and closing my palm over a star-shaped scar, I shake my head and remember why I'm doing this.

Clicking on my headlamp, I move into what looks like a sprawling sitting room, tripping on the rug as another guttural howl splits the air. Though I know the animal is far off, a shiver runs down my back. I feel like I'm being watched. When I turn back to the window, there's nothing there—though a flick of white fur between the trees confirms I got the wolf part right.

Worry less about the wolf and more about the mark, Sam.

Taking a deep breath of dust, I survey the living room with my red-tinted light, less visible from outside than the usual flashlight. Shit. The place is like a museum, complete with a gleaming grand piano and antique furniture that alone is likely worth millions. At the wall-to-wall mahogany wet bar, several dozen whiskey and scotch bottles preen in my light. I catch labels that can only have been bought directly in Scotland—at least a hundred years ago. Everything seems old, for that matter. Not just antique, but old-fashioned, like I've suddenly stepped into a different time.

On a whim, I hit one of the piano keys. It isn't dusty, but the sound is so out of tune, it makes me wince. A school music teacher once said that I had perfect pitch Actually, he said perfect pitch was wasted on me, but the concept's the same.

I let go of the piano key, my chest tightening. Something about this whole setup suddenly feels wrong. My gut yells at me to get the hell out, while my brain tries to talk down the panic. I'm already here, and it's ten thousand dollars.

And then there is another voice, a warm, coaxing whisper that brushes my mind, stroking my name.

Sam. Sam. Sam.

3

Sam

I twist around, my knife in my hand, ready to defend myself against… against what? My fucking imagination? Eyes moving, I stay very still, listening for any movement. Nothing. Only a nagging feeling in the back of my ribs, right at the spine. Shaking myself, I start up the sweeping grand staircase to the second floor. A jewelry box sounds like something one would keep in a bedroom, right?

The stairs creak beneath my light steps, spurring my heart to a faster beat. Stepping onto the carpeted floor, I pass all the closed doors on either side of the dark corridor and open the one at the very end. I go there first because it's where I'd put the master bedroom.

Not because something in there is tugging at me. Singing sweetly to me. Reeling me in with whispers of my name.

Because if *that* were true, I'd need to run out of here and check myself directly into an insane asylum.

Sam.

Pushing open the door, I feel a gust of cold wind biting my face.

Whoever came in to dust the piano without tuning it also left the window half-open. And there I was complaining about the poor quality of the downstairs window locks.

That feeling of being watched washes over me again, as it did outside the house. I twist around quickly, my gaze brushing past the four-poster bed. The carved armoire. The mirrored vanity. The—

The very large snow-white dog with yellow eyes who watches me from the corner of the room, a curious tilt to his massive head.

Shit.

My breath stops. *Don't run, Sam,* I tell myself desperately. *Move slowly. Very slowly.*

The dog blinks at me, then, with a decisive huff, thumps his tail against the priceless rug and lies down. Laying his massive head on his front paws, the monster seems resolved to simply observe my burglary.

I let out a breath of relief. A box. I need to find the box and get the hell out. Box.

Sam. As if summoned by my back-to-business thoughts, that whispering in the back of my head sounds again. *Sam. Sam.*

My heart jumps. This time, the whispers are louder and clearer than before, phantom hands pulling me toward the vanity. To the top drawer that slides open on silent rails with the slightest tug of my fingers, until a small iron box, covered with beautifully filigreed flames, fills the whole of my vision. I reach for it, cradling its heavy weight in my palms, a wave of contentment spreading through me as I reach toward the delicate clasp.

"Well done, Samantha." Ellis's smooth lilting voice, which is most certainly *not* inside my head, freezes me in place. His voice, and the sharp point of a blade pressed into the back of my neck. "Now, don't turn. Don't make a single move." The small sting against my skin increases as he puts pressure on the blade with one hand, the other palm extending into my field of vision. "Just place the box in my hand."

Right.

Swallowing a curse, I do as instructed—or try to, the *whatever*-it-is inside the box suddenly screeching desperately inside my soul. Not an angry screech, but a pitiful frightened cry, like a puppy abandoned outside in a rainstorm.

The damn box has an opinion. Given how this evening is going, I'm not even sure why I'm surprised anymore.

"Give it to me, Samantha," Ellis says behind me, my name rolling off his silken tongue, his warm breath and clean forest scent brushing my skin. "Don't get stupid."

No. No. No. The whimpering inside the box tears into my heart as I start to hand the loot over. I pause. The something whines with relief.

"Do you hear it too?" I ask Ellis, because why not.

He snorts derisively. "If I did, I wouldn't need your help now, would I?"

Oh. That clears it up. My left hand tightening around the box, I don't give myself a chance to think before I step forward and twist toward Ellis, slashing the nails of my free hand across his face.

He flinches—actually fucking flinches—his yellow-tinged eyes widening with shock as he fingers the thin red scratches now running down his cheek. Even now, he looks tantalizing, his pale hair glowing almost silver in the moonlight, his sculpted body the kind you can't just grow in a gym. His brows pull together. "How the bloody hell did you—no!"

His curiosity gives way to a sharp command as I open the box in my hands. Inside, a bloodred ruby sits nestled within a bed of black velvet, roughly the size and shape of a large egg.

I reach for it, and the gem purrs with happiness.

"Stop," Ellis barks, shoulders poised for a strike. Our eyes meet. Hold. His shift from yellow to an impossible metallic gold in the moonlight. "Do. Not. Touch it."

I swallow, my gaze taking in his tall, muscular body, every fiber in it coiled for battle. I've been hit enough times to know when there is no getting out of a blow, that this man has me in checkmate. My muscles brace, my breathing stilling in my chest as my back hunches slightly. I know exactly what's coming. That it will hurt. That I can do nothing to stop it.

And then I grab the ruby egg anyway.

The audacity of my choice is apparently as surprising to Ellis as it is to me, because the man's arm stutters, the knife skimming off my leather jacket.

I don't wait for him to correct his error.

Stuffing the ruby into the pocket of my leather jacket, I launch myself out the open window, taking my chances with a jump off a second floor over the probability of Ellis missing another blow. My pulse rises as I hang off the windowsill by my fingers, judging the drop and thanking whatever deity built the house on a hill.

Then I let go, hitting the soft grass with enough force to make the world blink—and just in time to see the flashing lights of half a dozen police cruisers pulling up toward the house.

Apparently, the alarm system works after all.

Fuck.

4

Sam

I am insane.

That is the only reasonable explanation I can come up with as I sit in Essex County's interview room, my left arm cuffed to a railing on the wall. The overhead florescent lights make the puke-green walls seem shiny, and I wonder who thought it would be a cheery idea to bother adding a white stripe accent to the color scheme. At least this room smells of bleach, which is an improvement over my cell.

"Ms. Devinee." Mr. Bryant, the public defender assigned to my case, straightens a jacket that's a great deal too expensive for a place like this. Large and suave, with thick, blond, gelled-back hair and blue eyes, he seems like he'd be unintimidated by any manner of client—not that I'm much of a threat. At a scant five foot three, my only advantage on the streets of Newark is that I'm freakishly good at blending in—and can fit in hiding places most bullies wouldn't even glance at. "Ms. Devinee, I need you to give me something to work with here. Something that's backed up with evidence. Whether or not you share their sentiment, the police like their evidence."

His accent is rich, cultured, with a faint hint of an upper-crust, like he was born in a well-to-do family. Most of the public defenders I've run across look ten years older than they are, with a severe coffee addiction and a heart way too big for their own good. This guy looks like he's never missed a wink of sleep his whole life, let alone brewed his own coffee. I gesture to his gold cuff links, my own cuffs clinking against the table. "I thought PDs didn't make any money."

"Ms. Devinee—"

"Family inheritance? Or maybe a side hustle."

Instead of losing his cool, he merely waits, one blond eyebrow lifted.

Impressive.

I tap my slippered toe again the table leg, which is bolted into the floor, the rough fabric of my blue-green scrubs scratching my skin. I wouldn't mind evidence myself just now, but try as I might, I have no explanation for what prompted me to try to steal that ruby a week ago.

Somehow "it asked me to take it" doesn't have the same ring to it the morning after.

"A man named Ellis promised me ten thousand dollars to break into what I thought was an empty mansion," I tell Mr. Bryant for the fifth time. "Except it wasn't empty. When I came to the bedroom, Ellis was there. He tried to kill me, but I jumped out the window before he could. That's when I got arrested. I gave the police Ellis's description already. And his number."

"The number you gave us led to a pizza place, Ms. Devinee." The attorney sighs, shuffling through the stack of paper in front of him. "As for this Ellis… I've looked over the police report. The police had the house surrounded and searched. There was no one else there except a dog who ran out the door and into the forest. Do you have an explanation?"

"No."

"All right. Let's go back to the evidence. Talk to me about the heroin, Ms. Devinee. I'm here to help you, and I can't do that if you don't talk to me. If you can tell the cops the name of your dealer, maybe wear a wire…"

My jaw clenches, my palm slamming the table. "If you want a name of a dealer, ask whichever cop planted the drugs on me. I don't sell narcotics, and I definitely don't put that shit into my body. I don't know how you want me to prove a negative."

Bryant straightens his papers, the task taking all his attention. "Ms. Devinee—Samantha—let me be up front with you," he says finally. "You broke into the wrong house. The owner is throwing everything at you, and he has the money to back it up. Your tox screen came back showing you were high as a kite that day—which, frankly, explains both the hallucinations about this Ellis and the half a kilo of product inside your jacket. If you would like me to go to the judge with 'a nonexistent man told me to meet him at an expensive house, drugged me, and planted heroin on me before turning into a dog,' I will. After which, you will be heading to federal prison with a mandatory ten-year minimum."

Bile rises up my throat as the world narrows around me. A part of me wants to cry, but I don't, clenching my nails into my palms as I always do to control my emotions. Finally, I raise my head to look Bryant right in the eye, because my pride is all I have left. "I notice the ruby is missing from the police report. Convenient for whoever took it from my pocket, don't you think?"

"No, Samantha." Bryant's tone hardens. "I'm done playing games. It wasn't a ruby, it was heroin. A very large amount of it. And if you aren't going to turn on your dealer—"

"I don't have a dealer. It wasn't my her—"

"Then you are looking at a life behind bars for a very long time. Do you understand me?"

My jaw tightens. Yeah. Yeah, I understand. I just can't do anything about it. I broke my own rule, trusted Ellis at his word. I took a job I shouldn't have. And now I have nothing. Not for me, not for Janie and Mrs. Leonards.

"Samantha, are you listening?"

"Yes. I understand. I'm screwed. Can I go back to my cell now?" My words are calm, but the need to run and hide in a dark corner as I lick my wounds is anything but. Fear and desperation course through my blood, making me hot and cold at the same time. My mouth is dry, my stomach clenching. I'm at my limit, and I know I'm going to break down anytime now. I just don't want it to be here.

Bryant's face softens. "There is one other option," he says quietly. "That's one of the reasons it took me several days to get back with you. I needed to see if you'd qualify. It's no more pleasant than jail, but it's only four years, and you'd come out with a new life. A new chance." Leaning forward, he braces his forearms on the table. "It's called Talonswood Reform Academy. A private rehabilitation institution. I may be able to pull some strings to secure your attendance."

I lift a brow. I've learned to look for the hook in men's proposals the way obsessed helicopter parents dig for razor blades in Halloween candy. A skill I should have remembered with Ellis.

"I am not a juvenile, Mr. Bryant," I tell him.

"Talonswood isn't for juveniles. The average first-year student is in his or her early twenties. But it isn't your typical school either. To begin with, enrollment means you agree to become a ward of the Academy, subject to its rules and discipline. Privileges to leave campus must be earned and often can't be obtained during the first year."

Bryant produces a sheet of paper which, though it comes out of a clear plastic folio, has the feel of thick parchment. The words on it are penned in the neat hand of someone who has way too much time to form pretty letters.

"This is the contract, which you'd sign and I would present to the judge on your behalf. You need to understand that there is no release clause. You may not simply decide you no longer wish to be there. Should the Academy decide to expel you before graduation, however, you would be going directly to prison."

"Ten years in federal prison or four at Talonswood." I grip Bryant's calculating gaze. "What the catch?"

"Talonswood believes that, given proper discipline, education, and opportunity, troubled young men and women can become highly productive members of society. The same cannot be said of many released inmates. Talonswood skews the results in its favor by selecting only candidates who appear to match the program. The most attractive part is what happens upon graduation—a new life. Many inmates reoffend after traditional prison because their pasts come back to haunt them. Talonswood will not have that. Call it witness protection without the witness part." Bryant smiles.

I don't smile back. He hasn't answered my question.

The attorney runs his fingers over the parchment. "Moreover, Talonswood has the funds to pay off students' debts before they enter the program and, upon successful completion, ensure that you have what you need to start a new life. Your record will be sealed, your baccalaureate diploma issued in a new name. Some of the students stay on to obtain master's degrees, and many return to teach."

"Sounds like paradise."

"Not in the least," Bryant assures me. "But I would propose that there are worse alternatives to be had."

Like the one facing me now. I swallow. There is a catch. There always is. But… Funds to pay off debts. Finagled correctly, I might parlay that into a year of home and bed for Janie. Bryant has hit a bull's-eye, and the sparkle in his eye says he knows it.

He wants me in Talonswood. I don't know why—or what's in it for him. But the asshole is right, the alternative is worse.

"Where do I sign?" I ask.

Bryant takes out a small knife and pricks the tip of his index finger, smearing the bead of blood over the finger pad before placing a bloody fingerprint on the parchment. Then he passes the knife to me.

5

Ellis

She'd scratched him. With her nails. And he'd bled like a human.

Bringing his practice blade down on a guardsman's shoulder, Ellis ignored the male's howl of pain. The male should have been faster with the parry, and Ellis was done treating the royal guard like a pack of pups. Spinning around, he blocked a blow intended to split open his skull, the force of the contact echoing through his bones. The guards were not pulling blows either. There was little love lost between King Bryant's guard and his bastard son.

Far above the training yard, a full moon ruled the evening sky, just as it had in the human realm. That was where the similarities between Talon—the immortal sanctuary that the fae carved out for themselves in the fae-vampire wars—and the mortal world ended. The humans' technology couldn't penetrate the portal membrane, just as Talon's magic would not flow back into the mortal realm. If Ellis never set foot in the human world again, it would be too soon. Bryant shouldn't have sent him there to begin with.

No matter. It was good to be back in Talon. Ellis was happy here

—well, not *happy*—he hadn't applied that word to himself for centuries—but he was comfortable. And he was away from the petite loudmouthed mortal who robbed him of his good sense, made him freeze on the job even before she'd broken his skin. He blamed it on her big hazel eyes, those mouthwateringly full breasts she tried—and failed miserably—to hide under baggy clothes.

So the witch was beautiful. Nothing he couldn't handle. She was still a bloody witch.

Kicking his second opponent in the chest, Ellis sent the guardsman tumbling to the ground, whipping his practice blade down toward him in a bone-shattering arc. Ellis was strong enough to shatter another fae's bones with a practice blade.

But even he couldn't draw blood from a fae male with a little clip of a fingernail the way Samantha Devinee had on his cheek. She made him wrong. She made him vulnerable.

"Ellis, enough!" The bellow came from the side of the practice ring, and Ellis blinked, realizing he'd been about to land a devastating blow on a male who was already down and clutching his ribs. Striding into the practice ring, the captain of the guard put himself between his downed underling and Ellis, mouth twisted under a thick black mustache. "Get the hell out of my training ring, Your Highness," the captain said, spitting on the ground. "I don't give a bloody damn that you are good enough to put down five of my males. I don't need a rabid wolf nipping at my pack."

Tossing his blade to the sand, Ellis stalked from the sparring ring. If the royal guard couldn't keep up, it was their problem. After spending eight months in the mortal world tracking down a little witch, Ellis had every right to burn off some fury. To do anything that might quiet his mind from the constant whispers of Sam's name, the memory of her citrusy scent making his head swim, no matter what he did. Not even the ire in his father's face when he learned how Ellis had botched the operation could shove the witch from Ellis's mind. That Samantha Devinee had no idea what she was somehow made it worse.

As if drawn by thoughts of his father, a servant appeared with a summons to the royal antechamber before Ellis was twenty paces away from the guard's training yard. Changing course midstep, he strode toward the palace without bothering to change, the neatly mowed moonlit grass dewy beneath his feet. The six immense white towers of the castle shone with glittering lamplight from every window, King Bryant's pristine influence stretching far over the land even in the dark. If the king didn't want to see sweat and blood, he could let Ellis be on his way. There was always some borderland to patrol, some stray vamps who needed killing.

That was Ellis's role in court after all, to go take care of whatever dark deeds needed to be done so everyone else could keep their hands clean. A royal assassin. A royal punisher. A royal bounty hunter. If it was a task the king didn't want to admit to, Ellis got it.

"I managed to clean up your mess, Ellis." King Bryant boomed by way of welcome as Ellis strode into the large study off his father's throne room, the gilded candelabra casting dancing shadows on the plush carpet. The king's blue eyes flashed. "I had to go down and do it myself."

Ellis stuck his hands into his pockets. "How verra inconvenient." It was his own minor little rebellion to hang on to the Scottish accent he'd picked up with his mother's family in the Scottish islands before Bryant decided to keep his bastard closer. The king's own accent had a North American cadence, just as did Asher's— Ellis's half brother. Another bastard and the only thing of Bryant's that Ellis cherished.

"It *was* inconvenient. Do you want to know how I did it?" He waited placidly for Ellis's answer, never lifting his eyes from the paperwork spread across his desk.

"So long as the witch is dead, I couldna care less for the details," Ellis said.

"I've pulled her out of what passes for a human legal system," Bryant answered as if Ellis hadn't spoken. "The Council would raise hell if I brought her here directly, but the witch will be on her way to Talonswood shortly. Not ideal, but best current option. We'll be able to keep a proper eye on her there, keep her out of the bloodsuckers' hands. Count Victor would love nothing more than a pet witch to do his bidding."

Ellis's stomach clenched. Talonswood Reform Academy—located on Talonswood Island where the gateway between the human world and Talon hung—would chew Samantha up, spit her out, and do it all over again. And that would just be in the first week.

The place was erected to get demifae and demivamps—and the occasional full-blooded immortal adolescent—under control, and made most bootcamps look like spa retreats. The enhanced strength and speed of immortal blood made such measures practical, but what would they do to a mortal witch? There weren't witches around anymore by the time the reform Academy was built on Talonswood, so Ellis never gave it much thought. Until now.

Though, for the life of him, he didn't understand why he *was* thinking of it now either. So long as the witch was nowhere near him, Ellis didn't care whether she went to Talonswood or the Arctic.

True, she'd be Asher's problem in Talonswood Reform—Ellis's half brother was the only horseman who still liked lost causes and was now the lead instructor there—but that was what the chump volunteered for.

Finally looking up from his desk, Bryant spoke with enough force to eclipse the room itself, his broad face twisted with cold fury. "You had one task—track down a witch so she could walk past the wards, have her retrieve a box, and bring the whole thing to me. I could have sent a bloody squirrel in your place for all the good you did."

Ellis clenched his jaw to keep himself from lashing out, the darkness inside him spreading with pulsating rage. Tracking down a witch with nothing to go on had been akin to threading a needle in the dark. After the witches exposed themselves to the humans a few centuries back, the race had been all but exterminated—the ones who remained didn't know what they were or what they could do.

For months, he'd kept his ear to the ground, listening for any sign of strange behavior, exceptional ability. Finally, murmurs. Whispers through the criminal network of a young thief for hire who seemed able to open any lock, do any job without detection, enter a building with only one blocked entrance and somehow find an exit. An uncannily talented young woman who had never been apprehended by the cops or incarcerated. So Ellis had traveled to the unlikely city of Newark, New Jersey. And waited. And waited.

Finding her at last—a small, round-eyed girl with messy red-streaked brown hair, torn skinny jeans, and the reflexes of a drunk toddler—had been almost laughably anticlimactic.

Yes, finding a witch was bad enough. But to go with only half the facts was insulting. Dangerous.

"You could have told me there was a damn egg inside," Ellis ground out finally when he could speak without screaming epithets.

"You didn't need to know what was inside." Moving faster than a male his size had any right to, Bryant crossed the room and gripped Ellis's throat. The strong fingers tightened like a vise that cut off blood and air as the king lifted Ellis off his feet. "But you can't follow simple instructions, can you? As useless a cur now as you've always been."

Ellis focused on drawing in the small stream of air he could, the world around the edges of his vision already becoming blurry. He knew better than to challenge his father outright, especially not when the bastard got it in himself that a reminder of the hierarchy was in order. If he were smarter, he wouldn't challenge his father at all. Unfortunately, Ellis had never been the smart one—that was his half brother, Asher.

As the world began to swim in earnest, Bryant let him go. Which should have been a relief, but wasn't.

"Why did you do it?" Bryant demanded. "You were supposed to slit the witch's throat, not let her open the box. Given your history with witches, I thought that would be the one rewarding part of the assignment."

Ellis's jaw tightened. The way "history" dripped from the king's lips so blithely, as if Ellis had merely had a series of bad romantic interludes. Not been held captive and tortured by a witch for ten years, along with Asher and the two vampires they'd allied with to try to end the species war, Reese and Cassis. The four horsemen, they'd called themselves. They'd thought it a clever jest. In the end, the jest was on them.

And yet Ellis didn't understand his body's reaction to Samantha either. Everything had been on track, the girl having passed the initial trial with flying colors. But the way the air had crackled when she had crept into the room, the tight dark pants and shirt accenting her perfect curves, had made Ellis falter. It might have been her eyes, the fire and rebellion in them burning bright enough to singe him, that made Ellis feel alive for the first time in centuries. Curious.

Even as he'd shifted from his wolf form, Ellis knew that the girl and whatever was inside that box belonged together—had been unable to deny them that one moment of connection before destroying everything. And after that, things got…out of control.

She scratched me, and I bled.

"I needed to know what I was dealing with," Ellis said, lifting his gaze to meet his father's even as he knew such impertinence could earn him more blood. "To know it was the right box at all. It was the first one she picked up."

"Of course it was the first one she picked up! The whole reason the damn urchin was sent there was because we thought she was a witch and could thus hear its call."

Ellis rolled back his shoulders, straightening his sweat-stained shirt. "So what's the problem now, Father? You have the box. The egg. You got to enjoy forcing me to skulk around the human world like some lost dog for months. Why are you still unhappy?"

"Because the bloody egg's imprinted on her, you idiot." Bryant rubbed his hands over his face, his jaw tight. "Whatever hatches from it, it's going to be tied to a damn witch now."

Ellis's eyes widened, the hot ire inside him turning to ice-cold rage. So that was the reason Bryant never told him what he was after—to ensure that Ellis felt no temptation to handle the relic. His father had wanted the hatchling for himself.

"You are going to fix this," Bryant said, and this time, the softness in his voice was deadly. "You deprived me of a hatchling, so you will break the handler to bridle. I hope you enjoyed your time in the human world, Ellis, because you are going to be spending years there. Four, to be exact."

No. *Hell* no. "Father—"

"And since you insist on acting like a pup with no brain to spare, you'll be treated as one. Asher has already received orders to enroll you as a first-year student. If you want to stay out of a dungeon cell, where you by all rights belong, you will keep the witch alive until she becomes competent enough to be useful to me, and you will ensure she learns obedience. Am I clear?"

6

———————

Sam

The black-tinted-out Suburban that stops to pick me up in front of the county jail looks like the kind of car they send for important people, usually with an armed driver. I'm sure the last part of that is true here as well. The officer escorting me looks skeptical as he speaks to the driver, but his eyes get a glazed look a moment later as he obediently hands over some paperwork and motions for me to get in.

Right. Point of no return. It isn't as though I didn't know it was coming, but somehow that step into the car feels much longer than the three feet it is, my chest tightening painfully around my lungs. I don't know where I'm going, whether this strange reform school is even in New Jersey. Or in North America, for that matter. Not that it matters. I belong to Talonswood Reform Academy now. Their latest delinquent to rehabilitate.

At least I'm out of those scratchy prison scrubs and back in my own clothes. My loose green cargo pants, cotton tank, and leather jacket have never felt so luxurious.

The driver honks at me, and I shift the backpack on my

33

shoulder—which effectively holds all the possessions I now have, including a homemade key chain from Janie and a letter from Mrs. Leonards promising that Joey will move out now that a stipend is coming. Then I open the door and slide into the back seat.

Which is not empty.

The fresh forest scent greets me right before simmering golden eyes meet mine, taking on a predatory yellow cast in the car's warm light. The man who tried to kill me two weeks ago now glares at me from two feet away. Dressed in black jeans and a gray V-neck that hugs his corded chest and biceps, his white hair loose and slightly mussed, he looks every inch the carefree rich bro—which I would believe if dizzying power weren't pulsing off him in waves.

I try to pull the car door back open, but find it locked. My heart squeezes, my hands tightening into fists. I might be a third Ellis's size, but I'm not going down without a fight.

"Happy to see me, I see," Ellis says, his tone no longer that of a suave gentleman but something rawer—darker—as if the man I met in the Lone Moon was merely playing a part.

"What the hell are you doing here?" I ask as the driver, hidden behind a tinted glass partition, hits the gas, launching the Suburban into motion. All of a sudden, unease gives way to fear, a slowly rising panic buzzing in my veins, the knowledge that there's more going on here than Bryant let on dawning on me with a sickening vertigo.

A muscle along Ellis's jaw tightens, and he leans one shoulder against the window on his side. The fancy signet ring he wore back in the diner is gone, a slight tan line showing where the band used to be. "Being punished. Because of you."

The panic has moved to my heart now, making it patter like a trapped rabbit's. But I keep my voice calm, level. "Let me guess, a posh attorney named Bryant sold you a bunch of shit on the virtues of Talonswood Reform?"

Ellis smiles coolly, his eyes as still and unreadable as stones. "Something like that. Though I usually call him something else."

I raise a brow.

Ellis's teeth flash in a cruel grin. "Father."

Fuck me. I pull my leather jacket tighter around myself and move as far away from him as the seat allows. Ellis is a bastard, but at least he's real—with the police and attorneys all assuring me that no one else was in the mansion, I was starting to believe them. "You'll understand if I don't shed tears that the man who tried to murder me two weeks ago managed to get snatched up by the cops too."

Ellis's eyes flash as if I just suggested he fuck his mother. "I'm not a man."

I blink. Not the words I was expecting. Before I can help myself, my gaze drops down to his pants—the sizable bulge beneath the black denim speaking for itself. "Could have fooled me."

"I'm a male." Ellis says this as if the word means more than it does.

"You are a backstabbing asshole who nearly cost me my life and did cost me my freedom. And the moment I get a chance, I am going to chop off your *maleness* with the dullest knife I can find and stuff it down your throat. Are we on the same page now?" My chest heaves as I spit the words, my body bracing for a blow. But I don't care. The words are worth a bloody lip or black eye. I don't think Ellis would go further in the Suburban.

He cocks his head, regarding me with a strange type of curious amusement and a tinge of infuriating pity—like I imagine the Big Bad Wolf did just before blowing the little pigs' houses to hell. "You truly have no inkling of anything. Who I am. What you are. Where we're going."

I raise my hand, unbending my fingers as I answer the three trivia challenges one at a time. "Asshole. Idiot. Prison."

Ellis snorts a laugh, the sound as dark as the tension swirling in his eyes. "That is remarkably accurate," he informs me. "Incomplete, but accurate."

"You have a better description?"

Ellis considers the car door for a moment, his chiseled face deep in shadow now.

"Don't sprain your brain."

"I was making sure the locks are engaged. It's too much trouble to explain when you can still run. But you can't now." He holds up his hand, the fingers long and probably powerful enough to crush my neck. Unbending his fingers one at a time just as I did, he enunciates the words with a self-satisfied vindictiveness that makes his words come out low and thick. "Fae. Witch. A place that will break you into a million pieces."

Witch?

"I didn't realize the Marine Corps ran an insane asylum." My words are light, but my whole body is prickling, my nerves jumping as if they too are desperately trying to get away from Ellis. He was scary enough when he was just a stone-cold killer, but as a *crazy* stone-cold killer, he's terrifying.

He's hazing you, Sam. That's all this is, one student trying to psych out another student before they even reach the gates. And yet... Unbidden, I remember that whisper in the darkness, echoing through the dusty halls of the mansion. *Sam. Sam. Sam.*

"I'd smart-mouth less and listen more if I were in your shoes, witch."

"Feel free to step into my shoes any time you like. Meanwhile, if you let me near a broomstick, I'll shove it up your ass."

"Next time you're holding a broomstick, I'll remind you of that," Ellis purrs, the words sending a shiver down my spine as if he's somehow in on a much deeper joke than I'm giving him credit for. With his sharp cheekbones sculpted in the playing shadows, he has a wolf-like look to him, especially when he smiles without humor and flashes a set of very healthy teeth. "Though by the time Talonswood has a crack at you, I don't imagine you'll have the strength to try."

"Aren't you worried that Bryant—or, wait, you call him Daddy —will spank you for telling me the secret truths? I presume he had his reasons for not doing so himself." Such as not being crazy and off meds.

"You signed away your freedom, you climbed into the SUV, you've nowhere to run. Safe to say your training wheels are officially off, Devinee." The sound of my name on Ellis's lips sends a ripple of heat through me, my blood speeding with a renewed cocktail of fear and anger.

My back straightens and I lift my chin, making myself as tall as possible, even if the top of my head only reaches Ellis's shoulder. This isn't my first rodeo. I know the rules, know that giving off at least the illusion of strength is vital. There is no surer way to be shoved to the bottom than to let anyone get a whiff of fear from you —well, other than crying, but that's obvious.

"You've been to Talonswood before, then." I snatch the piece of information from the air, tucking it away into a little pouch in the back of my mind. "The first time around didn't reform you enough to deter you from attempted murder?"

I don't see Ellis move until he's kneeling on the seat, his large body looming over me. *How did he—?* But all reasonable thought vanishes under the cold glare of his golden eyes. With one hand on the back of my seat and the other braced against the Suburban's tinted window, he has me trapped even without touching my skin. His musk brushes over my skin, making my thighs tighten even as my fists do. Damn. The man's body is so honed and lethal that I can't look away, can't help marking every coiled tendon. Or the dark, invisible weight that seems to press down on him from all sides. I swallow, my heart pounding so loudly that it echoes in my ears.

Ellis tilts his face down, his heat and scent slamming into me with the force of a storm. His full mouth is two inches away from me when he speaks, his voice is laden with menace. With a hate that can't possibly come from our short acquaintance, he says, "I'm not being punished for attempting to kill you, witch." Ellis's words pierce through me to grip my stomach. "I'm being punished for letting you live. And I regret it already."

Sam

blink at the sunlight streaming into the windows as a sleek sedan I have no memory of getting into pulls into the circular drive in front of a huge stone wall, a set of thick double gates with iron bindings as welcoming as the grim reaper. The gray columns rising toward the sky on either side of the entrance provide a perch for crazed-looking gargoyles, glaring down on the miscreants daring to enter. On all sides of the driveway, and lining the two-lane road behind us, dense forest shoots spiny arms into the darkening sky.

I try to take in clues to figure out where we are in the world, but I've never been far enough beyond Newark to make much sense of it. Trees, rolling hills rising into higher rocky-topped mountains, a chill in the air as the sun falls. In other words: the middle of butt-fuck nowhere.

Rubbing my face, I realize that my head feels heavy and that Ellis is gone.

What in the ever-loving hell?

I jerk upright, the full force of what just happened hitting me like a cold wind. The last thing I remember, we were heading toward Newark Liberty International Airport, the driver ordering Ellis and me to keep a civil tone in the back. And then… And *now* here I am, the sky overhead an unfamiliar pink hue that I think means dusk on the horizon.

"Did you drug me?" I demand.

The driver merely gets out and shuts his door in answer, walking around the back of the car toward my side.

"Yes, of course," he says, opening my door. For one very embarrassing moment, seeing him head-on for the first time, all I can do is gape. *This* is who's been driving me around for hours? He towers over the open door, broad shoulders backlit by the setting sun, a sleek black shirt hugging his muscled body like a glove. His dark hair is tied back in a ponytail, showing off a pale, sharply carved face, a face that belongs in a painting, not here in front of me with an impatient tilt to one brow. "I'm Reese," he says after a long beat, his crisp British accent belying the cold steel in his pale blue eyes. *This guy has killed people,* I know with sudden certainty. A lot of them.

I hold out my hand dumbly, which, instead of shaking, he uses to haul me up and out of the car with all the ceremony of a farmer throwing a bale of hay.

"I did not agree to being drugged," I say stupidly, swaying slightly on my feet. His scent makes me even dizzier, a delicious tang, like salty sea with a bite of mint. I inhale deeply before I can catch myself, making G.I. Joe actually lean away from me slightly, like whatever kind of crazy I have might be contagious.

"Did you think I'd be handing you a map and welcome packet to a place we very much prefer no one ever finds?"

Or runs away from.

"Where's Ellis?" The words spill out before I can stop myself. The man—male—whatever—might be an asshole who deserves to have his balls cut off, but at least he's a familiar face in all this.

"Less talking, more moving, Samantha." Reese's tone is hard, something in his eyes when he looks at me that feels personal, almost like he hated me before even meeting me. "The lead instructor will answer your questions. Or not. It doesn't matter to me." Though everything said in that clean British accent of his has a way of sounding polite, there's no mistaking the note of command. Reese is military. Or was. From the way his eyes are always moving, his body seeming ready to kill even when standing still, I wager he has a special forces tattoo somewhere on that pale body of his.

Gripping my backpack, I walk toward the forbidding stone entrance, feet crunching loudly against the pavement, forcing myself to keep my head high as if the world is mine for the taking. As if my heart isn't racing despite the number of times I've been shipped off to live in one place or another, whenever a foster family decided they were tired of me or wanted to take a vacation without some street kid hanging on. Or, my favorite, when some male of the family decided I wasn't paying my keep and decided to take their chances that the next foster girl would be more willing.

More desperate.

Except I'm not a child anymore, and, though being dumped in a new place with no explanation still makes my gut churn, I'm not about to let it show.

Sticking my hands into my deep pockets, I turn around in a circle inside the gates, taking in the high gothic buildings lining the four sides of a vast, empty green that must be at least an acre across. Lights are coming on in windows, perhaps students just coming back from their last class. Here and there, dense leafy trees cast slanting shadows in the golden light. It's almost…idyllic. Maybe my next four years won't be such a shitstorm after all. Not after Newark. "So this is Talonswood? Cute."

I see the movement in my side vision a second before a boy's hand clamps around my throat, lifting me onto my toes as a rush of sudden panic courses through my blood. I claw instinctively at the grip, my hands sliding off his cool skin as if it were polished leather. I gasp for breath, kicking my toes against the ground to get purchase.

"Cadets do not speak unless spoken to, *witch*." The boy's cruel dark eyes glare at me, the specks of orange in them flickering in the sunlight, his black widow's peak sharp enough to cut glass. As he gives my neck a shake, I can smell the stench of raw meat on his breath. "Am I clear?"

"Let her go, Quinn." Ellis's command, coming from somewhere behind me, is a quiet menace that makes my attacker's lips pull back in a snarl. "Or I will dismember you joint by joint."

Quinn throws me down to the grass and steps back, turning on Ellis. "Who are you to give me orders, *cadet*." Quinn's face darkens. "Your royal sperm donor isn't protecting you now."

Ellis growls, looking like he's about to leap—but stops when he sees something behind me. Or someone.

"Well, that took all of five minutes," a low voice says.

I struggle to my knees and turn. The golden-haired man walking toward us across the grass draws all the fight out of Ellis and Quinn as if popping a balloon with a pin. Though he only looks to be in his midtwenties, somehow he carries the air of someone far older and far more in control. Before Ellis can open his mouth to say anything, the man raises his palm and settles his eyes on me. I know I'm holding my breath, know I should release it, but can't find the muscles to do so.

"My name is Commander Asher," Golden Hair says in a calm I-can-kill-you-with-my-bare-hands cadence, the shape of his eyes an echo of Ellis's. *Relatives?* But if Ellis holds himself like a wolf about to pounce, Asher is like the predator who is busy surveying his territory. Cold. All-knowing. In control. With Asher's posture military straight under his blue uniform, I wonder if he and Reese served together.

"I am the lead instructor here, as well as acting headmaster while Dean Javin is away. Cadet-Commander Quinn is the highest-ranking cadet at Talonswood Reform and the only full immortal in the student body. And you've met Reesand, my lieutenant. You'll meet the rest of our faculty in the coming days. Together, Reese, Quinn, and I are your commanding cadre—the officers in charge of your class. Whatever any of us tells you, you will execute that command as if it came from a divine source. Understand?"

No. "Perfectly."

"Sir," Quinn snaps.

"Perfectly, sir," I echo back like a parrot.

Asher looks at Ellis.

"Yes, sir," Ellis says with a mildness no one here is buying.

Asher sighs almost reluctantly. "Quinn, three lashes to Ellis for speaking out of turn to you earlier."

My eyes widen, the small glint of satisfaction flickering over Quinn's face somehow more frightening than Asher's offhand order. It's all I can do to keep from flinching when Asher turns toward me, his broad shoulders and handsome face making my breath hitch for many reasons at once.

"Ms. Devinee, as I truly hope you are aware, you are now a ward of Talonswood Reform Academy. You may call this a reform school, a military prison, or hell on earth—so long as you do it out of my earshot, I don't care. What I do care about is that you understand that our rules are strict and absolute."

"I un—" I start to say, shutting up as Asher shakes his head.

"No, you do not. But you will." He nods to Quinn. "Take Ellis to the post and then meet us at the hose. Samantha, follow Reese and me."

I spare a glance for Ellis, who seems both unsurprised and unfazed by what's about to happen to him, and then hurry to follow Asher as instructed. *Dammit.* Despite myself, I already fear making the man angry at me even more than I fear crossing Quinn again.

Quinn is like mean miniature Dachshund. Asher is a wolf.

Holding on to the strap of my backpack, I walk between Asher and Reese, the two instructors bracketing me like prison guards. I wonder if this is how all new students are welcomed, or if I'm just extra special.

Witch, Ellis's voice spits in my memory as if in response, making me shiver.

Quinn has said as much too.

I swallow.

As we angle right across the dusky green, tall wrought iron lamps come on along the walkways, and we finally pass other students for the first time, paused to watch the procession. I try not to stare, but it's hard—so hard. The girls, dressed in blue plaid skirts and white button-downs, all look cut out of the pages of *Seventeen* magazine, tall, willowy, smooth skinned, with silky hair down to their butts, in every natural color of the rainbow. Not dyed hair like mine—I can tell immediately that none of them would ever be so crass.

The boys, in blue blazers, are all athletically built and as beautiful as the girls, some with porcelain-pale skin like Reese's, some with a feral angle to their eyes like Ellis's.

I thought these were supposed to be a bunch of juvenile delinquents. What do they put in the water here? Fuck. Maybe I'll wake up with muscles and hair down to my butt too.

When I meet the cadets' gazes, the dislike in their eyes is palpable enough to leave a bitter aftertaste in my mouth. In foster care, another brat meant another threat to what little anyone had, but no one here looks underfed in the least. Nor does Talonswood appear to be lacking in anything but common sense. The four fortress-castle-mansion things could probably fetch enough money to buy a small country, their stone façades in perfect repair, even the ivy growing in seemingly intentional patterns. The metal fences at the corners of the yard are no less gorgeously elaborate, the wolf-head designs on them works of art—and their currently open leaves ready to swing shut. To turn the large green into a grand prison yard in a matter of seconds.

"You are the only witch at Talonswood, Samantha," Asher says abruptly as we bend around the rightmost building to stop at a piece of soggy ground behind it under a single harsh spotlight, the forest rising darkly in the background. "The demis do not know what to make of you. Frankly, neither do I."

Demis? Yet another word that sounds like gibberish. "That makes all of us," I mutter. "What does being a witch mean exactly? Should I be able to fly or do magic or turn men into toads?" My pitch rises with each word until a hard look from Asher silences me at once.

"No. Potentially. No." Asher tells me curtly, raising his hand to stop further inquiries. "You will learn more in class. Let me be clear

—you are welcome to protest, cry, question the truth all you want, just do it on your own time." Asher is hiding his emotions better than Quinn had, but something unkind flashes in his eyes nonetheless. "I will not abide bad behavior under my watch. You *are* a witch, a nonhuman species. That carries risks to all two— apologies, three—creature races. I do not expect you to know what I am talking about yet—I do expect you to spend your every waking moment learning."

For the first time, hearing it in Asher's cool, logical voice, my brain has a hard time rejecting it. It's impossible. But when you hear something enough times… I think of cauldrons, frogs, pointy hats, and somehow know that's not what it means.

My chest tightens for a moment at the memory of the purring ruby, a deep longing for it spilling into my blood before I blink the nonsense away.

"Demifae and demivampires are products of imprudent pairings with unsuspecting humans, who usually find themselves with offspring they cannot control. Worse, if the human was compelled by the vamp beforehand, they end up with no memory of how the child came to be or who its other parent is," Asher says without looking at me. I listen to him numbly, barely able to take it all in. "As a result, most demis themselves don't know what they are until they create enough problems to get the Council's attention and land themselves here, sponsored by the full-fae and full-vampire communities respectively."

Ah, sponsored. That begins to explain the glossy entitlement oozing from them. Fuck. Not only are vampires and fae real, they have damn trust funds. It would all be morbidly funny if it wasn't happening to me. My pulse quickens, and though I try to listen to Asher, pulling air into my lungs is suddenly an effort. This can't be real. A dream. Or a high. Except I don't do that shit. Did someone—

"Samantha?" Asher's tawny eyes are very real. And very fucking pissed at having caught me with wondering thoughts.

"I'm listening, sir," my well-developed sense of self-preservation replies at once.

Asher nods. "The demifae come believing their powerful bodies and quick healing are products of their gym excursions, while the demivamps credit their superior intellect instead of compulsion as the reason behind people doing their bidding. Talonswood sets those things to rights and ensures all creatures' obedience to Council law."

"Council?" I say, shutting my mouth quickly as I remember Quinn's warning and see Asher's eyes flash in displeasure. "Sir," I add quickly, not sure if I'm making things better or worse for myself.

No, of course vampires and fairies are real. Of course there are half-magical assholes running rampant around the world. And of course there's a Council of higher-up magical assholes ruling them all. Who was I to think I needed more information?

Asher's lips press together, making his stern face look even more devastatingly perfect. "In short, the Council enforces basic rules of creature conduct in the human world. There is more to it, but there will be time for history and civics later." Bending down, Asher picks up the garden hose that seems responsible for the wet earth, flicking the water on with his thumb. "For now, put your things down and strip."

"Are you insane?" I wheel on him in time to see one blond eyebrow rise. "I mean to say, are you insane, *sir*? Because I can get you a straitjacket if you'd like."

Asher turns on the hose, aiming the frigid water straight into my chest. "My record at standing here with a cadet is ten hours," he informs me, voice as cold as the water. "But please, make it twelve. Unlike you, witch, I'm immortal and have all the time in the world."

I gasp, choking on the spray, my hands coming up to cover my chest from the icy onslaught. He can't be serious. He can't be. Breath hitching, I stare at the two males standing fully clothed before me, their legs spread wide apart in a steady stance that is so at odds with my own curled-in shoulders.

"We have company." Reese jerks his chin behind me, and, just when I think the moment could get no worse, I see Ellis walking toward us, golden eyes seeming to gleam impossibly through the encroaching dark.

A tight look I can't read passes over Asher's face as he points to a spot right beside me, repeating the same order he just gave me. "Strip."

I wait for Ellis to balk, secretly glad to have someone else fighting against insanity, but the male is already pulling off his gray V-neck. Wet cloth slides off a body a sculpture would envy, revealing that the lithe hard muscles I saw on Ellis's forearms were only the start. Tanned skin stretches over the eight hard ridges of his abdomen and hugs the pointed crests of his hips, which flow into corded thighs and—I try and fail not to notice the large cock anchored between his legs.

My face blazes as I realize the man has caught me looking and now grips my gaze with a nonchalant amusement that makes me long for the earth to open.

Right up until I look more closely at said earth. At the fact that the water running off Ellis's back is tinged red with blood.

Holy fucking hell. The gravity of the place I've gotten myself sent to crashes down on me with enough force to make me stop breathing. I picture Janie's face—the reason I took Ellis's job and Bryant's deal, the reason I'm here, learning truths about myself I'm not even sure I want to know.

And still, I would endure far worse than this to keep Janie out of harm's way.

As Asher's spray of water returns to me, I find my hands moving to the zipper of my leather jacket, then the hem of my tank top, my cold fingers fumbling on the clasps of my bra as I strip bare before the cadre who now owns my life. As the new world of Talonswood closes its vise around me, I cling to one desperate mantra.

Don't feel. Don't feel. Don't feel.

8

Asher

*A*sher put his hands into his pockets, his stance casual as he leaned against the bay window of the common room in the instructors' suite he shared with Reese. At least he hoped to hell he looked casual, because inside, he felt anything but. Even as he gazed out at the darkening sky, all he could see was Samantha Devinee, her furious hazel eyes, her cargo pants hanging on the crests of her hips as she finally pulled off her shirt. Her heavy breasts as she pulled off her bra, rosy nipples peaking in the cold as if begging to be sucked. Never. Never in his life had he looked at a naked cadet with anything but cool detachment.

Now it felt like his body had betrayed him. And he hated Devinee for it, whether it was truly her fault or not.

Though the little witch barely reached Asher's shoulder, she took up space. Too much space. Certainly enough to set Asher's cock pulsing painfully, as if he was some colt, not yet grown into control of his primal urges.

Of course, he'd been expecting to feel things when he met her—

the first witch he'd laid eyes on in four hundred years. Oh yes, he'd expected to feel lots of things, none of them nice.

And that was what made all of this twist his insides so tightly. It was wholly unacceptable. Not only was Sam Devinee a cadet, she was a witch. After what had happened to him and the others at the hands of a spell caster, that in itself should have made Asher enjoy watching her torment.

Instead, all he'd felt was irrational fury as he got the full view of the round scars of cigarette burns crawling along her arms, of the other marks wrapped around her too-thin body. Seeing what state the cadets showed up in was most of the reason Asher had instituted that particular intake procedure, though it had the side benefit of setting the tone of who here was in charge. Talonswood cadet residents didn't end up here by being model citizens—they got snatched up for causing enough trouble among humans to get the Council's attention.

Except Samantha. She'd been the victim, not the bully, hadn't she? Of her birth, of her own unfortunate beauty—too tempting for the scum of the world to ignore, no matter how hard she tried to cover it up with loose clothes and hair dye—of King Bryant's scheming, of the ancestors who were no longer around to guide a young witch to a power locked inside her.

Ironically, as much as he'd dreaded her arrival, the petite spitfire Samantha Devinee was the one person in the whole Academy who had done nothing wrong, even if the red streaks in her brown hair betrayed her rebellious nature.

Red. Asher's jaw tightened.

Like the crimson that had run from Ellis's back for crossing Quinn over the damn girl. Quinn was an ass who Asher couldn't get rid of, but to have to order the snot-nosed brat to whip Ellis sent a new dread spiraling through Asher's gut. The witch had not been at the Academy a day, and already there was blood seeping into the ground. She pitted creatures against each other without even trying.

Hell take him, Samantha's mere presence was pitting Asher's own body against him.

That was the problem with witches.

It wasn't fair. To her, to him, to anyone. Barely over twenty, the girl didn't even know creatures existed, much less that she was one of the last surviving members of her species—but that didn't stop the trouble she brought with her. And it would not stop Asher's nightmares of what a witch had done to them from getting a rerun in the coming nights—or Ellis's or Reese's, he was willing to bet. Luckily for Cassis, the vampire ran a high-end club off campus and wouldn't have heard about her yet.

Asher snorted. It was the first time the four horseman were together since Sienna's torture chamber four hundred years ago— and it, once more, involved a witch. The bloody irony was not lost on him.

Let's not overstate "together," Asher reminded himself. Ellis and Reese hated each other, and Cassis cared for no one. Not anymore.

Though Reese has stayed silent as the witch stripped, Asher knew the vampire was just as displeased about a witch's arrival. Beyond displeased, most likely. When it came to females, Reese got... bristly. Asher suspected that Reese's frequent stints in the human special forces were simply the surest way of staying away from the female of any species.

With a sigh, Asher turned toward the sound of approaching footsteps and grabbed two glasses and a bottle of good whiskey from a shelf. Ellis was going to need a drink.

"You are not supposed to be in the cadre quarters, *cadet*," Asher called over his shoulder, setting down the bottle just as the door opened behind him. Extending Ellis a filled glass, Asher shook his head at the blue cadet's uniform his half brother now wore, his pale blond hair dripping wet. "Are you all right?"

Taking the offered drink, Ellis downed half of it in one gulp before slowing to savor the full-flavored taste as he sat down on the couch. "Hell, this is good. Is the bloodsucker here?"

Asher nodded toward the door to Reese's room and sat. It was bad enough Sam had walked into his world and set it on its ears, but now to have Ellis here under his watch... "About Quinn earlier—"

"It was the right call. I mouth off, you punish me like anyone else, even if it was practically a child holding the whip. I don't imagine today's order will be the last one you issue." Ellis lifted his chin in challenge. "Unless you've gone soft since your navy days? Did you exchange the cat for a time-out?"

Ignoring the taunt, Asher poured them both another drink. Asher had no problem ordering discipline—it was the norm among immortals, and he'd personally ordered it more times than he could count when he'd led human armies of less modern time. But this was different.

Ellis had broken himself many times over to keep Asher alive when Sienna captured them, and this new status of Asher being his brother's senior, it wasn't how such sacrifices were repaid.

But Ellis was right. He'd known the cost of insulting Quinn and had done it anyway. Because Ellis was just self-destructive enough for that. Fucking hell. They were all broken toys. Deadly. Honed. And broken. "At least let me see your back."

Ellis savored another sip of his drink. "I have a runny nose. Will you wipe that for me as well?"

"What am I supposed to do with you, Ellis?" Asher snapped, setting his own glass down on the table. "Run you around with the rest of the first years when you can decapitate half the Academy's cadre without breaking a sweat?"

"That's my understanding, yes." Ellis started to shrug but stopped, stiffening almost imperceptibly. The male could refuse to admit that he felt pain, but he did. "If you want details, ask Dad. So long as I keep the witch alive, that fulfills my sentence—and I have a very loose definition of alive. I can't tell you how little I care what happens beyond that." Ellis lifted his glass, speaking over Asher's shoulder. "Oh, hello there. I can't say I've missed you. I'd worry we would be having a full-on reunion, but I presume Cassis at least is too busy entertaining his cock to bother me."

With a sigh, Asher looked up to see that Reese had stepped out of his bedchamber and now stood with one forearm braced against the doorframe, dark hair loose to his shoulders, his other hand holding a glass of blood.

"I smelled blood." Reese took a slow sip from his crystal glass. "Fae blood, I mean. And iron. Quinn took an iron tip to you, didn't he? We don't allow those to be used on our fae cadets normally, but then, you aren't one to tell. You probably enjoyed the hell out of it."

Ellis snapped his fingers. "Reesand. Now I remember—I meant to bring you some straws. I've seen several decrepit humans sip their dinner that way, and thought of you immediately. Hunting is sooooo… Crude, after all. Chewing too."

Reese growled, stepping forward into the room with his chest out just as Ellis rose from the couch. The vamp, who usually lost his temper over nothing short of world war, now stood with nostrils flaring, Ellis's face dancing with amusement.

"Enough with the bloody monkey dance." Getting between Ellis and Reese, Asher shoved the males apart. They had bigger problems. Unlike fae and vampires, the witches were mortal and able to practice outright magic in the mortal realm. That Samantha Devinee had no idea *how* to cast anything didn't mean she couldn't. She'd be a valuable weapon in the wrong hands, including her own, once her power was unlocked. The Council had been content to let Asher run Talonswood, but it wouldn't stay that way now. And once the creature hunters caught wind of the news, they'd be lighting pyres.

Life would have been easier if Ellis had just killed her. Maybe Asher wasn't all that sorry for having him whipped after all.

"What are we going to do about the witch?" Asher asked.

That got the others' attention, Ellis returning to his spot on the couch after refilling his and Asher's glasses and pouring a third glass for Reese.

"I dinna know what *you* are going to do," Ellis said, his words dark with echoes of a different time as he braced his forearms on his knees, "but it's my fault Devinee is here, and my job to keep her alive." Throwing back the rest of the whiskey, he put the glass down and headed out the door. "Like I said, however, I have a very loose definition of alive."

9

Sam

Carrying a stack of starched white shirts, way-too-short plaid skirts, and blue PE gear that Reese silently handed me after he and Asher had their fun, I walk through the lantern-lit hallways of the first-year-cadets' barracks, skirting around a set of four students on their hands and knees hand-polishing the hardwood floor. The girls make no effort to kneel modestly in their short skirts, showing flashes of silk underwear that I'm sure are intentional. Given the fancy gold-leaf murals along the walls, Talonswood can clearly afford more efficient cleaning methods—which makes this special blend of luxury and humiliation a deliberate choice.

"Witch crossing," one of the boys stage-whispers as I pass, his foot snaking out to catch my ankle.

My whole stack of uniforms splays over the damp floor as I land hard on my hands and knees. Swallowing a curse, I collect the clothes calmly without giving the boy the satisfaction of my anger— and stop at the sight of a large boot holding down the last of my skirts.

Looking up, I find myself staring at the sharp black widow's peak at the top of Quinn's face. "Throwing your clothes off already?" the cadet commander says. "How…unsurprising." He crouches to get on the same level as me and holds up the skirt with two fingers. "Don't worry. You'll be on your knees soon enough."

I recoil, but Quinn is already up on his feet, striding over to critique the efforts of the cleaning crew. Gathering all my stuff together, I finally find the stairs and follow the numbers to room 216, as indicated by the slip of paper Reese likewise forked over. A piece of paper. Not a key.

Because students at Talonswood don't get keys to their own locks.

Stopping before 216, I find the nameplate bolted to the door, the small clear compartment fitting two name tags: *Bernadette Yalls— demivampire,* embossed on thick metal in the top slot, and *Samantha Devinee—witch* scribbled in marker on a slip of lined paper below.

I wonder whether my arrival has deprived Bernadette of her single. Glancing over across the hall, I see Ellis's name marking the door right across from mine. There is no second person on that door. My stomach tightens for a moment, my brain trying and failing to convince itself that having a gorgeous would-be murderer within arm's reach is somehow a good omen.

Rapping on the door twice—and getting no response either time —I give Bernadette until a count of five before letting myself inside and surveying my new cage. Unadorned white walls, a light lilac scent in the air, two narrow windows—no curtains, which I'm assuming means no sleeping in. The furniture looks like a lopsided Lego set, with one each of the two identical beds, writing tables, bookshelves, and drawers shoved into a corner like discarded rubbish.

Sitting behind a writing table on the other side of the room, a girl with a long red braid glares at me over her shoulder, her green eyes flashing with that snarl I know well. *Keep your hands off what's mine.*

"I'm Sam," I say, smiling—might as well.

"Yeah," Bernadette says in a high, velvet-smooth voice, turning back to her work. "I've fucking heard."

I shrug, dumping my stuff on the floor and pulling out my old flip phone to try Janie. She'll be out of her mind with worry by now, probably thinking I'm dead in a ditch somewhere.

"Don't bother," Bernadette says without turning. "No internet or cell service off-island for students." Finally, she turns back around to flick a single chilling glance down my body, from my dripping leather jacket to my baggy camo-green cargo pants with a hole in one knee. "Not that I expect anyone's waiting desperately for your call anyway."

Right. Time to set some ground rules. Grabbing my writing desk —which is currently pressed flush against my mattress, so that I'd have to sit on the bed cross-legged just to use it—I shove the wooden thing right into Bernadette's drawer set.

"What the hell?" Bernadette is on her feet at once, her braid whipping behind her, intensifying the lilac scent. She's taller than me, her body a perfect hourglass of smooth curves and lean muscle. In her leisure wear—silk periwinkle booty shorts and a matching lace-edged camisole—she looks like an off-duty Playboy Bunny. "You don't touch my things, witch. You don't so much as look or breathe on my things. Understand?"

Stepping around her, I grab the foot of my bed and drag it into position to claim more floor real estate. "Keep your shit out of my space, and we won't have a problem."

"This isn't your space." Bernadette's foot stops my bed frame. "And let me be clear, by *this space*, I don't mean my room, or even Talonswood. I mean everything. The world was cleansed of your kind once, and no one here is eager to see a cockroach return."

My kind. She means witches. At least I seem to be catching on to that much.

Knowing better than to ask Bernadette to explain, I shove my clothes into drawers and climb into bed, turning my face to the wall as the day finally crashes down on me. I'm cold and I'm exhausted, and in the past twenty-four hours, I've been drugged, stripped naked, and lifted off the ground by my neck. I still don't know what being a witch entails, beyond giving everyone carte blanche to shove me around. It's enough to make anyone cry a bit in the dark.

But I don't. I'm tougher than that.

~

I WAKE to the ear-piercing wail of a siren, Bernadette kicking my mattress as I sit up like a jackrabbit and look out the dark window.

"Get your ass dressed and to the parade grounds," my roommate orders, grabbing a workout uniform from my drawer and throwing it into my face. In the hallway outside, feet are already starting to pound toward the stairs. "We are not getting punished on account of your being late. Quinn imagines himself joining his sire's court after this year, and I swear his power trip will kill one of us before the term is through." She mutters this last part with an unmistakable note of jealousy in her tone.

"What time is it?" I ask, pulling on my sweatpants while Bernadette slips into her kit like some kind of ninja. The dark sky outside the window shows no sign of dawn.

"Which part of 'move your ass' needs extra explanation?" Bernadette demands, her braid whipping behind her as she stalks to the door, where a stampede of blue pants and T-shirts is already heading for the stairs.

Try as I might, I can't help marking Asher's golden hair and broad shoulders as he presides over the exodus in crisp fatigues, a stopwatch in his hand. As if catching me watching him, Asher lifts his tawny gaze to meet mine for a moment before turning away.

My thighs clench, a jolt of heat coursing through my veins despite my common sense.

Shoving Asher firmly out of my mind, I spill out into the green with the forty or so other inmates—err, cadets—who are already lining up in formation under harsh spotlights, their uniforms clinging to lean, perfect bodies, as if Talonswood only reforms special forces dropouts.

Well, them and me.

Speaking of special forces—my breath catches as Ellis strides out the door, his long, sure steps overtaking the others without actually seeming in a hurry. If I thought he looked hot in nice clothes, the tight red Under Armour T-shirt hugging his biceps turns him from model to predator—a red T-shirt that is decidedly *not* the plain blue uniform the rest of us are in. Surveying the gathered cadets and instructors with a general's eye, Ellis cocks his pale head a bit as if making a mental note before coming to stand beside me.

"Are we meeting your expectations, Master Ellis?" Quinn croons.

"It's your formation, Cadet-Commander," Ellis answers, the polite words lined with enough steel that I wonder whether the two know each other or if Ellis is simply self-destructive enough to bait a man who literally took a whip to him yesterday.

I shiver, the combination of yesterday's memories and the night's cutting wind making me shift my feet.

Turning from Ellis to me, Quinn presses the tip of a thin rattan stick he carries under my chin. Lifting my face up to his, the cadet-commander smiles down at me, his orange-tinged eyes glazed with a mix of disgust and cruelty that makes me freeze.

"Tell me, did you dye your pussy the same red, witch? Better yet sh—"

"Quinn. If you please," Asher calls from the front of the formation, making a muscle in Quinn's jaw twitch as he walks away from me. Clicking off his stopwatch, Asher shows the digits to Reese, who stands with hands draped loosely behind his back, hair pulled back with a leather thong, black joggers and T-shirt fitted perfectly to the hard angles of his body.

Reese shakes his head.

"Welcome to fire drill, first years." Asher's call cuts across the group, the students on all sides of me remaining perfectly still, faces forward. "The bad news is that you are three seconds slower than last week. The good news is that your cadre will be giving you plenty of chances to practice in the coming months. First, however, we've two new problems joining this mess of a class. Ellis of Talon and Samantha Devinee." Asher nods to the pair of us. "Ellis is of fae heritage. Samantha is a witch."

The cadets shift from foot to foot, a rustle of whispers spreading through them like wildfire. The sudden movement is almost shocking after their robot-like stillness. On all sides of me, faces turn, every shade of surprise, disgust, even hatred playing across them. The girl on my right takes an exaggerated step away from me, as if I might carry the plague. Only Ellis remains still.

I guess it's safe to say they didn't all know about me yet. Which means the fun is only just getting started.

"Lock it up," Quinn barks, tapping that rattan rod of his against his thigh. The cadets go silent and straight with almost comical speed.

"Given the historical violence and hysteria surrounding witches, and the ongoing vigilance of creature hunters," Asher continues, "the following additional safety measures are instituted starting now. One—nightly fire watch will now be conducted in pairs. Two—unannounced drills such as the one entertaining you this morning will double. Three—the afternoon defensive combat will be increased by one hour. You are not here on vacation, people. Anyone caught so much as thinking of violating Talonswood rules will be punished—and trust me when I tell you that you will get tired of the experience a great deal sooner than the cadre will."

Another wave of whispers rushes through the formation, the angry glances shooting in my direction sharp enough to slay. My fingers curling over my palms, I meet each and every one of them, though I know, deep down, that I have no bite to go with my bark.

"Silence," Asher snaps, and though he is obeyed instantly, a growl that sounds like a pissed-off Doberman rumbles from his chest. "Mister Quinn, it seems the class has some issues to work through before regular training. Will you oblige us with a fun run to help them do that?"

Snapping his fingers, Quinn takes off at an ankle-twisting pace, the cadets falling in behind him in an amorphous group that sweeps

Ellis and me along in a wave of morning misery. Well, my misery. Ellis seems to be enjoying the run.

As I double over a mile and a half later to lose what little contents my stomach has in it, I realize that Bryant never mentioned whether all the students who enter Talonswood actually live till graduation.

1 O

Sam

The first run sets the stage for my first week in Talonswood with the skill of an artist's brush. In addition to being the only witch, I'm apparently the only one who can't run for shit, a pastime which everyone at Talonswood considers both a virtue of the highest order and a sign of intelligence. Sure, there were times I had to escape quickly on the job, but since I was so good at hiding, that rarely meant running for any period of time. Turns out I have no cardio—which would be funny if there wasn't already an enormous target on my back.

After watching me fall out less than fifteen minutes into the first run, Asher sends me off to learn how to hand-wax floors for the rest of the morning and makes me redo the run alone with him instead of having breakfast.

I run no better then. I just do it for longer.

Some of the students forgo breakfast too, just for the fun of standing along the edges of the green and laughing into their coffee cups.

Between bouts of failing at every physical training exercise and polishing my menial labor skills, I listen to vampires and fae lecture about the history I've never heard of. Of Council laws forbidding the supernatural creatures—namely fae, vampires, and witches—from holding positions of power within human society or otherwise bringing attention to themselves.

Apparently, the last time that happened, it triggered the Spanish Inquisition, which exterminated most of my kind.

My kind. A strange concept after a lifetime of being an orphan, passing through the filthiest corners of the foster system—a concept that sends a tiny tendril of pain in my gut if I think too hard about it. Which is why I try not to. It's crazy to waste time missing what I never had, and anyway, the other witches would probably reject me even if they were here. I have nothing resembling magic.

Except for that ruby thing.

Shaking away the memory of that night, I make myself focus on Reese's current lecture about how, witch problems aside, the fae and the vamps had been at each others' throats for several thousand years. The conflict came to a head in the sixteen hundreds, when the fae-vampire wars for control of Talon broke out.

"To make a long tale short, the fae won," Reese says, his tone academically smooth, though his body looks ready to turn to cold-blooded rampage at a moment's notice. "They control Talon and the gateway to get there, while the vampires remained restricted to the human world. In addition to housing the gateway between worlds, the island of Talonswood has been declared a neutral ground for all creatures. Many vampires congregate here to recreate a sense of community or power that they've lost." Reese's gaze slides over Ellis, who is sprawled at his desk with a bored-looking expression.

For a fleeting moment, the two males exchange a meaningful glance that, for reasons I can't understand, makes my heart ache for them both. Ellis's hand tightens on the edge of his desk.

"Isn't that under debate, sir?" The boy who tripped me on the first day, a beautiful olive-skinned demivamp named Christian, with traces of a French accent, smiles smugly. "Staying in the human world allowed the vampire clans to dig their roots in. Clans such as

Count Victor's may not have palaces, but the reach of their actual influence spans the mortal world—which is quite a bit larger than Talon."

Turning to Christian, Reese raises his chin. The motion is almost imperceptibly small, but still makes the cadet shrink into his chair. "Nothing I say is under debate, Christian."

Christian swallows.

"The bottom line to remember," Reese's piercing blue eyes catch mine, even though he lectures the class, "is that witches have always been the only ones able to use true magic in the mortal world. Certainly, the fae can shift to animal form and are difficult to injure without iron, while vampires' speed and compulsion abilities fall into the realm of what humans would call supernatural. However, these things are simple extensions of our bodies. Yes, Bernadette?"

"Is there a way of checking if someone is really a witch or just claims to be?" my roommate asks sweetly. "I heard that true witches have one spot on them that doesn't bleed. Does Talonswood have a protocol to test for that? It would be a shame, after all, if someone accidentally allowed a human into our ranks and we'd then have to kill her just to keep our secret."

"I volunteer to put such a protocol into practice," Ellis says. His words are light, but the fleeting tension in Reese's face says there is more to the quip than I think.

When the bell rings a moment later, Reese dismisses us to lunch without further comment.

Grabbing my books, I stalk out of class, pausing to watch second-year demifae trying to shift into animal form on the green. Most will never succeed, but it's the ones who can't control themselves that the instructors worry about—they call them weres, as in werewolf. As if this place wasn't already terrifying enough. I hear the woods around Talonswood have cages of feral wolves, tigers, eagles, and more, deformed and monstrous, uncontrollable.

Shuddering, I continue on, my thoughts swirling my mind at hurricane speed. Bernadette might have intended her question as petty torment, but the girl had a point. Walking into the mess hall, I head directly for where Ellis sits alone and pull over a chair.

"What do you want?" he asks, cutting into a piece of meat that barely saw a fire, much less touched one, before being put on a plate.

If I had any appetite after Reese's lecture, I'd have lost it at the sight of Ellis's lunch. "How did you know I was a witch?" I ask.

"You mean without having resorted to seeking your witch mark?" Ellis raises a brow, his golden eyes sharp. Strong fingers plunge a fork into the meat. "I used the one tried and true method of gathering information—I paid you."

"You paid me to take pictures of some files from some old attorney's office."

"Old being the operative word." Ellis puts down his fork, bracing his forearms on the edge of the table as he looks down at me with flat eyes, taking up all the space and air in the room. "The file I had you photograph was behind a basic lock spell keyed to witches. From a time long ago, when such things were common. A nonwitch would never have been able to open it."

"So you, what, went through everyone in New Jersey until you found the one unicorn who could pass your test?"

"Everyone in America. And I did a little better than that. But what is it that you're really asking me, Devinee?" Ellis leans closer, his sculpted face dangerous. His lips so close to mine that his warm breath brushes my skin. His fresh pine-forest scent makes my head swim. "You want to know whether you really are a witch?"

I swallow. "Yes."

Ellis smiles without humor. "You tell me. What happened when you walked into that house? What drove you to open the locked box when I had a knife to your neck, to wrap your hand around a ruby when everything sane inside you must have been yelling for you to run? Was it magic?"

I learn forward hungrily, sensing answers. "What was that ruby? Why did you want it?"

He pulls away instantly, eyes suddenly flat on the wall opposite him.

"Why did it get you landed here?" I press.

"That ruby responded to your power. And that's all you need to know for now."

I slam my palm on the table, the wooden top wobbling slightly. "So where is that power now? Why am I as weak and useless as I've always been?"

Ellis steadies his coffee, which, judging from the smell, is well spiked. "I neither know nor care," he says, his eyes never leaving mine, something like hatred swirling in their depths. "But for all our sakes, I hope you never find it."

Brilliant. I stand up, pulling myself away from him. The more I observe the male, the less I understand him. The less I understand why he let me live that day.

"Devinee," Ellis says, catching my wrist, the skin contact—his hand callused and warm, almost pulsing with heat—making my body tense. "There's a nightclub called Dusk on the southwest side of town. Ask for Cassis and tell him you're a witch. He may have answers for you."

I frown, studying Ellis's face, looking for any clues in the chiseled lines around his mouth, the high cheekbones, or steel-wall eyes. But his face gives nothing away. "Asher said we were not to leave the Academy quad, even during liberty."

"It isn't a rule the cadre enforces. But...if a threat of a possible beating is enough to keep you down, maybe you don't want your answers as badly as I thought you did." Releasing my wrist as if it were suddenly made of fire, Ellis leaves his lunch unfinished and walks away.

Ellis

He was supposed to be enjoying this, Ellis reminded himself as Sam doubled over on the side of the running trail, her breath so ragged, he could hear her wheezing. The tight blue shirt hugging her breasts steamed with sweet sweat that rose into the air, the pants stretching around her backside reminding Ellis of just how very much a female Sam was.

And also that she was officially the worst runner Ellis had ever seen, even among the humans. A week into Talonswood's training regime and Sam couldn't run half a mile without stopping. By the mile mark, the girl was full-on losing whatever food she had in her stomach.

Ellis shook his head just as she pulled herself back up and onto the trail, twigs and pine needles sticking to her knees. Given the witch's pace—and the five-mile morning running course—it should take, oh, two hours or so to get back to the parade grounds. Even Quinn had gotten bored with this reality and stopped riding her after the first day.

"I've spent centuries in and out of the military, but I think this is the first time I'm starting to wonder whether dying from a run may truly be possible." Asher, who'd been backing the group, came up beside Ellis just as Sam tripped over a tree root and went sprawling onto the trail again. "Not that we can call that running, even charitably."

"She has no immortal blood in her." Ellis didn't know why he was defending the witch.

"I'll be sure to mention that to anyone coming after her," Asher said. "And by anyone, I mean that the Council is making a visit."

Ellis turned his head sharply. There were six members on the Council: three vampires and three fae, the three remaining witches' seats empty for lack of the species. "Javin?" The fae male was the official dean of Talonswood Reform, but had been content to let Asher and the other leads run their cohorts as they saw fit while he pursued personal machinations. Talonswood Reform existed because it had to, not because anyone actually wanted to spend time putting the demis into place.

"Count Victor."

Ellis cursed. The vampire has been one of the leaders in the fae-vamp wars and—despite respectable appearances—was unaware that the war ended.

"The demivamps are already bending over backward to conjure ways to impress him, just like the demifae do whenever our dear old Dad decides to make an appearance," Asher continued. "The bastard Victor encourages it, dropping hints through Quinn that he might consider inviting some half bloods into the clan."

Just what these already cutthroat demis needed, another bone to tear each other apart over.

Ellis cut his gaze from Sam, who was bracing her arms on her thighs as she pulled desperate gulps of air into her lungs, and back to Asher, the male's line of conversation finally making sense. The witch was a novelty, and with the demivamps tripping over themselves to show off before Victor, she would be a prime target.

"If Samantha doesn't get better quickly, she's going to get hurt," Asher said, nodding as if he'd read Ellis's thoughts. Both Bryant's bastards, Asher and Ellis had been born only a month apart, which gave them a shared understanding of each other that was usually reserved for twins. Or had, before one witch broke them all, leaving bloody pieces of their soul for the crows to pick at. "She has not a drop of immortal blood and less natural ability to fight than a beagle. The demis will tear her limb from limb and not even notice."

Ellis's chest tightened around his ribs, the same way it had when Quinn had grabbed Samantha's neck. Worse still, he saw a mirrored look in his brother's eyes. "She's a witch," Ellis reminded them both, his wrists aching beneath the phantom weight of long-gone shackles. "So long as they don't kill her, I don't care what the demis do."

"I grew up with you, Ellis. I bloody know when you are lying."

"With due respect, sir, keeping the cadets at bay is your job." Ellis gave his brother a mock salute. "I'm just here to help when the hunters decide to come calling, because we all know they will. Well, that, and to be appropriately humiliated."

Asher quickened his pace, cutting in front of Ellis and stopping.

Catching a spark of triumph in his brother's tawny gaze, Ellis crossed his arms over his chest, his gut warning him that Asher had just led him into a trap. "Asher—"

"Oh, no, you don't." Asher rocked back on his heels, throwing a quick look over his shoulder to where Samantha was trudging ahead with painful slowness. "Seeing how you are, as you said, under my full command, I have some new orders for you. Father wants you to keep the witch alive. I want you to do one better than that. Help her keep herself alive. You are now promoted to pack leader with exactly one cadet beneath you." Asher jerked his thumb toward the witch, a corner of his mouth lifting as Ellis's nostrils flared with sudden ire. "Get the witch in shape. Running, fighting, the works. I can give you a month before I put her in hand to hand against the others, but that's as far as I can stretch it."

Ellis's fingers curled into a fist, the willpower it took to keep from driving his knuckles into his brother's nose no less than the witch was exerting. Yes, Asher had set him up expertly. And Ellis had fallen right into the bloody trap.

Asher's face hardened, his gaze dropping to Ellis's closed fist. "Don't."

Drawing a breath, Ellis forced his fingers to relax. He little feared punishment, but it would hurt Asher to order it more than the male deserved. Even for this. "Orders received and understood," he said instead, the words clipped but proper enough. Without waiting for a response, Ellis moved around Asher and closed the distance to the problem he'd just inherited.

A problem that was now down on one knee, swallowing a whimper as her calf seized up with enough force that Ellis could see muscle bulging beneath blue cloth. This was supposed to be the pleasurable part, damn it, watching the witch flop around like a fish on dry land. But somehow, Ellis couldn't find pleasure in it at all. And that pissed him off.

"How did you survive as a burglar when you can't run a hundred paces without losing your lunch?" he asked.

"Go to hell," Sam said through clenched teeth, red-tipped brown hair sticking to her pale cheeks.

"We are both already here." Ellis let a cruel smile spread across his face. Despite his still-simmering anger at both Asher for setting up this trap and himself for falling right into it, Ellis's mind was already assessing his newly inherited disaster. Once, before a witch named Sienna changed everything, he used to enjoy training armies —not that his trainees shared the sentiment at the time. Leaning close enough to Sam that he could smell her sweet and citrusy scent, Ellis brought his mouth to her ear. "Though I'm about to make it feel even more hellish for you."

It was oddly satisfying to see the blood drain out of Sam's irritatingly beautiful face.

1 2

Sam

"What the hell?" I oomph awake as something heavy lands on my chest. Ellis's unreadable face hovers a few feet away. For a second, I think he barged into my room and smacked me as some form of deranged hazing, but then I realize that the weight is still there, and it is bag shaped. I glance at the window, not even surprised to find that dawn has yet to visit. On the other side of the room, Bernadette's bed stands empty, my evil roommate busy with fire watch. Not that she seems to need much sleep.

Sitting up, I push the bag off me. "What is this?"

"Your new training gear." Ellis leans against the doorframe as I open the smooth zipper to find a whole slew of things inside. Under Armour and Lululemon shirts the same color as the Academy uniform, but of higher quality, wrestling shoes, a set of boxing headgear and gloves, a weighted jump rope. Even a fluffy towel and lavender-smelling shampoo.

The bag itself is quality, and everything has that things-from-a-store smell, the kind that doesn't cling to Goodwill donations.

Pulling out one of the jackets, the tags promising to keep its wearer warm even in rainy weather, I can already see it will fit me perfectly. I haven't had anything this nice in my life. "Where did you get this?" I ask.

"I conjured it from thin air. Where do you think?" Ellis crosses his arms over his chest, his biceps straining against the sleeves of his black training tee, and I'll be damned if the sight doesn't send heat racing down the inside of my legs. "It's bad enough you can't walk ten meters without tripping on a good day. Your body is a damn lilac when the weather is bad."

I glance at the still-attached price tags, my brows climbing. Each one of those little tight workout shirts is over fifty bucks, and the neon-yellow Nike sneakers are north of two hundred. Yeah. Closing the bag, I throw it back at Ellis's chest. "I don't need your charity."

"Good, because you aren't getting it." Ellis hurls the bag back at me like a hot potato, his Scottish tones taking on a more rolling brogue with anger. "But in case you were too deaf to hear yesterday, there has been a change of plans, courtesy of our all-knowing and powerful cadre. I'm training you until such a time in the far-distant future when you are able to find your own ass with your hands without a map, GPS, and three guides. And I am going to have enough problems dealing with you without also having to work with what this Academy calls gear. Change and let's go."

I drop the bag onto my bed and pull out a set of training clothes and shoes. Realizing that Ellis is still there watching me, I raise a brow.

He merely leans deeper into the doorframe, a sardonic tilt to his brows. "You think you have something I've not seen before?"

"That doesn't mean it's open season on my naked ass." After closing the door in his face, I pull on the first new set of clothing I've ever owned —I was right; each piece fits perfectly, including the cool max sports bra, which I don't even want to think about the male purchasing—and step out into the hallway. "All right, what is it we're doing? After all, I can barf with the best of them in almost any circumstances."

Ellis gives me a dark look that sends a warning shiver down my spine and motions for me to follow him as he moves through the night with predatory ease. I shiver when we get outside, but not as bad as usual, the thin high-tech jacket and thinner base layer doing their jobs as advertised.

Instead of heading toward the forest trails or stopping at the usual dirt-packed training corrals behind the north castle, Ellis leads me into a long, low outbuilding beyond them. After climbing down a set of narrow stone stairs, we walk into what turns out to be a bona fide gymnasium with things like punching bags and training mats and a cage in the center that would make any MMA fan drool. Harsh overhead lights bely the usual old-fashioned flickering-lantern vibe of the dormitories and classrooms. It seems they choose modern or Dark Ages depending on what suits their cadet-torturing needs best.

The whole thing makes my stomach sink.

"Headgear and gloves," Ellis calls, beckoning me into the ring. He himself wears only the fingerless grappling gloves, his skull apparently too hard to worry about something as insignificant as a strike from me. Or, more likely, the male is simply certain that I won't land—

I stumble back as Ellis's fist hits the side of my head, my whole body bucking with the force of the assault. "What the hell?" I yell at him. If I hadn't just clicked my headgear into place, I'd be seeing darkness right about now. "I wasn't even—"

The second strike comes before I can finish my sentence. I stumble, nearly losing my footing from the force of the blow, a dull ache spidering through my side. My heart quickens as I see Ellis move again, my hands rising.

"I'm sorry, were you expecting an embossed invitation?" Ellis says calmly, not a hair out of place on his blond head as he circles easily around me.

When the damn male goes for a third strike, I feel something inside me snap, fury spilling into my blood like a fine cocktail. Teeth grinding together, I launch myself at him and shove him in the chest. Hard.

My palms connect with rock-hard muscles that might as well be a stone wall, the collision bouncing me onto my ass.

Ellis smirks at me.

My world darkens at the edges, my body focusing on one overwhelming need: to bury my fist in Ellis's perfect fucking face. With a snarl, I step in again, aiming my knuckles right for his nose.

This time, instead of letting me land the blow, he blocks the swing midmotion and hooks his foot behind my heel. I fall flat on my back, my whole body hitting the harder-than-it-should-be foam with a resounding thump. A moment later, he follows me down and mounts me, straddling my midsection with powerful thighs. His forest scent surrounds me, not a hint of sweat in it. For him, this isn't even a warm-up.

"What the hell do you think you are doing?" he barks into my face, his eyes dark.

I don't answer, the roaring inside me too loud to process his words. I'm trapped. Held down on my back. My heart pounds against my ribs, my breathing fast and hard. I can't be here. Not again. I'm not going to be here. At any cost.

Nails out, I swing wildly at Ellis's eyes, my hands a blurring windmill between us.

Ellis growls as he snatches one of my wrists, pinning it expertly against the mat. "In what world do you imagine that flailing like a bloody maniac is going to get you anywhere?" he bites out, emphasizing his point by forcing my elbow up, the joint lock sending pain exploding through my shoulder.

I swing at him with my free arm.

Ellis's face hardens, the pressure on my shoulder increasing until I have to clamp my jaws together just to keep from howling. The asshole is going to rip my joint apart.

"Lesson one," he says, his perfect face merciless as he looms over me, his blazing eyes showing me a hint of the Scottish warrior I'm sure he used to be, many moons ago. "You don't flail like a fish on dry land. You think. You orient. Now, tap out, and we'll start again."

I glare at him, breathing through the pain and panic and my racing pulse.

"Tap out," Ellis enunciates, as if I'm either hard of hearing or too much of a dimwit to understand quite so many syllables strung together. "That is when you acknowledge your surrender and I let you up. It is how this training is going to work."

"Like hell I'm surrendering to you," I say through clenched teeth, my shoulder howling in pain. It isn't as if Ellis doesn't know what he's doing to me, that the power to hurt or release me is fully in his hands. I hate him for it. But I'm not going to beg for mercy.

"Tap, snap, or nap," Ellis orders coolly, not letting up on the pressure. "The choice is yours."

And I'm making it. I'm not begging for the pain to stop like some weakling, throwing myself on Ellis's good will to let me up. That's what he wants—that's what they all want, and I learned long ago not to give it to them.

"Are you truly going to make this a problem?" the male demands, and this time when he increases the pressure on my shoulder, my pained scream fills the entire concrete-walled gymnasium, echoing from the high walls.

Ellis lets go in disgust. "Lesson two," he says as he climbs to his feet, looming over my limp body. "You do what I say when I say it. Closely followed by lesson three—if you don't tap out, you are going to have an even longer day than you do already."

13

Sam

By the first day of liberty, ten days after my arrival at Talonswood, I don't care how much trouble I'll get into for leaving the cadets' quad and heading into the small town. I just need to get away from Ellis. If we had any televisions or computers at Talonswood, I'd think he must have watched every one of those marine training movies with dick drill sergeants and was now moving down the list of every torment known to man.

Except, of course, being an immortal fae male, he has a much larger and more extensive list of techniques than Hollywood could ever come up with. In the past three days, he's literally doused me with freezing water before forcing me through calisthenics in a sand pit, made me bear-crawl the running trail, and thrown me fully clothed into the deep end of a twelve-foot pool to introduce me to swimming. The only thing he hasn't done yet is take one of those rattan canes to my shoulders the way I saw Quinn do.

Maybe Ellis knew that would be a bridge too far. Or maybe he alphabetized his torment and we haven't made it to "W" for whippings yet.

For my part, I've thrown up, passed out, and half downed. But I haven't cried.

Which I think might be pissing him off. I fucking hope so.

With his perfect body exuding power without even trying, his every movement filled with leashed violence, the male deserves a little irritation now and then.

Tugging my leather jacket closer around my uniform blouse—which is the most presentable top I own—I try to shake the annoyance that thoughts of Ellis now provoke in me with Pavlovian predictability and quicken my stride through the picturesque streets of Talonswood. Getting out of the quad proved easier than I'd expected, a quick scramble out the window and down the rough stone wall. I might suck at running, but climbing out of windows—that I'm good at.

Or, more likely, Ellis was right that the "stay to the quad during liberty" rule is more of a formality. Given that the place is on an island, with miles and miles of forest surrounding the habitable part (that much Reese told us, though he didn't specify where in the world we are), running away isn't an option. Which also explains why no one is bending over backward to make sure I stay locked up like a good little delinquent.

Talonswood Reform Academy, I quickly discover, makes up only a small part of what could best be called an immortals' university town, a small enclave in the human world where it seems vamps, demis, and whatever fae chose to stay out of Talon can be themselves. The town has an old-world charm, almost like a postcard of some European city, with winding cobblestone streets lit up with tall iron lampposts and small white-painted brick buildings with colorful awnings and potted flowers. I see some humans as I walk too—they stand out like red flags, with their short, weak bodies and hair that's not straight out of a shampoo commercial. Reese mentioned in class that they live and work knowingly alongside immortals, some passing the secret through generations, others simply liking the pay and knowing how to keep their silence.

I wonder how many humans, the ones outside Talonswood, know about the existence of creatures. Certainly someone must.

The government? Is this one of those things they tell the president along with nuclear codes? *Here is your briefing on the Middle East, sir. And here is another one about a magical realm you didn't know was even a thing.* I wonder what the new presidents say to such news. I wonder what Janie would say if I ever get the chance to tell her. Which I probably won't. Those were the rules. For a moment, I miss the girl so deeply, I can't take another step.

Then I make myself shake it off, burying my emotions deep in the back of my mind. I did right by Janie coming here. And that will have to be enough. Letting that resolve wash over me, I start walking again.

Outside the red-brick-and-ivy academic quarter, there's a small but very posh residential area, a bustling commercial strip where the nightclub Dusk is located, and tons of huge, very fancy buildings that look dedicated to various forms of research. Oh, and vampires. There are a lot of vampires.

They look at me with open curiosity, even something like lust, which makes me shiver. Unfortunately, for once, I'm not dressed to avoid this kind of attention—I don't know who this Cassis is, but I'm beginning to get the sense that vampires have little tolerance for frumpiness. I'm wearing my best skinny jeans, black and skintight, tucked into chunky black ankle boots. The white lace cami under my jacket is little better than a nightie, for how much of my cleavage it shows. My hair is loose, and I light-fingered some of Bernadette's mascara and eye shadow for good measure. It's the best I could do.

And when I open the heavy door of Dusk, the nightclub Ellis told me to go to, I can tell immediately that it's not good enough. I almost step right back out onto the street. For something that looks so shady from the outside, Dusk is the most upscale club I've ever seen. Gleaming walnut floors, a wall-to-wall bar with lit-up shelves of liquor that must be worth more than most people's cars, and thong-clad dancers decorating six pure-white marble pedestals. Their polished skin and long, swinging hair glow in the low light, fangs unsheathed as they smile alluringly at the patrons, male and female alike. And just in case you can't get a good look at the girls from where you are, each of the dancers is also projected on the large-screen televisions hanging like lust from the high ceiling. I'm not into girls, but even I think they're hot.

Strobe lights sway along to the music, slowing down to settle on a man sitting just behind the shiniest Steinway grand piano I've seen, even on TV. My mouth waters with longing. With short dark hair and a black Italian suit cut to perfection, the man caresses the piano keys with a lover's anticipation, the background music quieting instantly as he brushes the first note.

The sound vibrating through the air makes me freeze, every nerve in my body strained toward it. The man's long pale fingers race over the keys with a mix of practiced precision and fiery passion that makes the whole club hold a collective breath in deference. His gorgeous, sharp-boned face remains relaxed, only his dark eyes betraying his concentration. Fucking hell, I could listen to that piano for the rest of my life and be happy.

"Well, look who strayed far from the nest." A hand cups my jeans-covered backside and squeezes hard. I'm turning around before I can judge the wisdom of it, my fist heading straight for the groper's nose.

The man catches my wrist easily, his bald head and leather biker jacket both reflecting the colorful overhead light. Large and ugly, and more than a little drunk, the man yanks me toward him, fangs already half-unsheathed. "There's a reason you little caddies aren't allowed at Dusk."

Yeah. Ellis never mentioned that part.

I try to knee him, for all the good it's doing. "I'm here to see Cassis," I snap, trying to make it sound like a threat. Though, given Ellis's setup, Cassis might be a bloody pet newt for all I know.

The man snorts. Apparently, I said something funny. "And why do you need Cassis?"

I swallow, the piano continuing its song, the chords coming faster than before. My heart quickens, my body writhing to get away. "None of your business," I snarl, filling my lungs to scream. I'll make a scene if I have to. "Let me go or—"

The man's dark eyes catch mine, his irises turning from brown to black as the pupils dilate. My body stops moving, my mind suddenly sluggish, hazy.

"Explain what you want with Cassis," the man repeats, his tone so deep that it fills my whole skull, gripping it like a toxin. Words tumble from me, the words I've been wanting to say since Ellis first dangled the hope of answers before me.

"I'm a witch. I heard Cassis could help me."

The music stops, the temperature in the whole room suddenly dropping several notches. The man who captured me tosses me roughly to the floor. When I look up, the back of his hand is raised high, the knuckles having already marked my face for a target.

My heart pounds, my shoulders hunched for inevitable impact. Idiot. I was a fucking idiot to believe Ellis.

"Hal," a smooth, powerful voice, like a river rushing over stones, cuts in from just outside my vision. "Let yourself out. You know the rules about touching girls."

My attacker steps back at once, his palms rising into the air. "Cassis, she said—"

"I heard." The speaker steps into view and grips Hal's gaze. It's the piano player, even more terrifyingly beautiful standing over me than he was sitting at the Steinway. "Get out," Cassis snaps, that rushing river of a voice turning into a tsunami.

Hal's already pale face blanches further, his boots scraping as he retreats toward the exit mumbling things I can't make out because Cassis now turns his attention to me. He wears a dark red shirt, the liquid silk as rich as blood, the collar unbuttoned enough to reveal the top of a muscled chest. The well-tailored black suit he wears over it has a Versace logo, the cloth hugging the taut body in just the right places to make my chest tighten with more than just fear. As for his face...

I swallow as I meet high cheekbones, a sculpted jaw, and rich brown eyes, the lashes so dark, they look painted. But I know they're not. His beauty is as real as the power pulsating around him like lingering notes of a piano.

"Show is over." Cassis raises a hand and waves, the single motion sending the frozen club right back to their dancing and conversation, the DJ kicking off recorded music. Looking down at where I'm still kneeling on the floor, the man adjusts one of his golden cuff links, his dangerously gorgeous face as unreadable as the rest of him. "I imagine someone played a joke on you when they sent you here," he says, his clipped British tones reminding me of Reese's, spiked with cockiness. "You aren't a vampire."

No shit.

"Dusk isn't for you. Go back to school and find yourself a pack." He cocks his head. "Unless, of course, you are really a witch."

I get to my feet. "And if I am?"

Cassis gives me a devastating smile that never touches his dark eyes. "Then you will never have a pack. You will never be safe."

Yeah, well, tell me something new. I raise my hand in a mock salute. "Right. Sorry I disturbed your music."

Cassis's gaze catches my eyes, the brown in his own darkening just like Hal's did. "*Leave.*"

"Yeah, interview's over. I got the message." I flash him my middle finger and snort at his sudden confusion. Maybe no one has ever dared to flip Cassis off before. Then again, there might be a very good reason for that—one that I shouldn't wait around to discover. I start toward the door.

"Wait."

"Indecisive much?" I turn, finding Cassis staring at me with renewed interest. Like a wolf watching an unusual little porcupine. "What?"

Cassis's eyes grip me again, their color changing to darkness. "Spin around for me." His murmur drops to a lower seductive orbit that makes my sex clench. "Let me get a good look at that gorgeous ass."

"Right. We are done." I take a step back, inwardly cursing. I'm going to kill Ellis. I will fucking work out a way to do it.

Cassis grabs my chin, his cold fingers and expensive musky scent sending a shiver through my body. "Fascinating."

My heart jumps, my muscles waking to action.

"Relax," Cassis orders, his eyes wholly black as he releases me but stays close. Too close.

I shove him in the chest with all my strength, which moves him not an inch but knocks me back several steps—right into a tall table with a bottle of cognac and several priceless crystal glasses. At least they certainly sound priceless when they—and I, and the table—all crash to the floor, the ring of shattering crystal as pure as the notes of Cassis's piano. As the piercing pain reaches my brain, I realize that I didn't just break several glasses, I landed right on them.

A thick trickle of blood covers the heel of my hand and wrist, running onto the floor and soaking the bottom hem of the white lace cami I'm wearing under my jacket. When I raise my hand to examine it better, several soft hungry growls sound from around the room. A moment later, I realize the crowd is slowly closing in on me, all eyes on my wound. On my neck. On my blood. The brunette dancer runs the tip of her tongue over her sharpened canines.

A shiver runs down my spine.

"She's mine," Cassis snaps, and the entire crowd takes an instinctive step back.

When Cassis extends his hand to me, I'm smart enough to take it, something telling me that I'm not walking out of Dusk in one piece otherwise.

1 4

Sam

The music rises to new volumes as I follow Cassis out the back door behind the bar and up a well-lit staircase to a softly illuminated landing above the club. Cassis opens the door, standing aside to let me into a vast modern flat, floor-to-ceiling windows showing the full expanse of the night sky. As in the club downstairs, there's a bar with top-shelf alcohol at one end of the room and a grand piano beside that. For some reason, the piano makes me feel safer, as if music can somehow protect me.

In the center of the room, sleek brown leather couches surround a heavy marble coffee table whose iron-clawed legs curl in a design that reminds me of a woman's body.

"I had those commissioned especially for my den," Cassis says, his accent making everything sound just a little more polished than it has any right to be. He strides over to the bar. Given the resemblance between upstairs and down, I'm fairly certain Cassis actually owns Dusk. "What do you drink?" he asks.

Whatever's cheapest. Usually water.

"Never mind, I'll surprise you." Taking out two glasses, he fills one with scotch and the other with something thick and purple and fruity smelling. I get that one.

Taking the drink in my good hand, I squint at the writing on the bottle my drink came from and roll my eyes. "Cassis. You poured me a cassis liqueur."

"It's as close as you'll ever come to having me inside you," Cassis says. "I couldn't deprive you of that little."

I put down my drink, the tiny sip I took tingling the inside of my mouth. Cassis liqueur is thicker and stronger than I expected. And the fact that I just thought those particular words, even in the privacy of my head, is wrong on so many levels.

Cassis grins.

"Right." I help myself to a cloth from his bar and wrap it around my hand. "You don't want me here. I don't want to be here. So how about you take me out the back door like a hooker and we call the evening quits."

"I take my hookers out the front door," Cassis informs me, his dark hooded eyes telling me that he's only half kidding. He's still standing, towering over me like a predator. "And you can't leave. You broke a very valuable bottle and glasses. You owe me."

My jaw tightens. "If I had any money, do you think I'd be going anywhere dressed like this?" I motion to the bloodstained white cami about two sizes too small for my breasts, and my tight black jeans, wearing through in one knee. "These are my *nice* pants."

"No, I don't imagine you would." A corner of Cassius's full mouth tugs slightly. "But there are ways around it."

Oh, so this is how he wants to play it. My pulse jumps, my eyes darting to the door he forgot to lock after letting me in. If I move quickly enough—

"Didn't I already tell you that you are getting no closer to feeling me inside you than my namesake there?" Cassis sits himself across from me on one of the leather couches and crosses one ankle over the other knee, the fine Italian weave stretching over his muscled legs—and the bulge between them. I do everything I can not to look at it—and fail. "You can work it off. I need a bartender."

"No, you don't."

He shrugs a shoulder, watching his drink swirl around his glass before taking an indulgent sip. "Mmmm." He licks his lips. "True. But I want one. And seeing as you've no other way of repaying me, it seems you're hard pressed to say no."

I throw up my hands, wincing as my injured arm moves more than it should. The mixed signals coming from the man are starting to drive me certifiable. Ellis must be having a great laugh right now. "Why?" I demand, as if I have any standing in this conversation. "I seem to remember clearly you wanting to throw me out of Dusk and onto my ass less than ten minutes ago."

"But you didn't go," Cassis says, as if that's supposed to explain something.

"Is that a novelty for you?"

"It is." He lifts a dark brow.

I look at the door again, knowing I should be a great deal more scared than I am being alone in this man's—male's—flat. Yet there is a strange kind of fascination that keeps me here too, a dull tug deep in my core.

Or maybe there's nothing strange about it. Let's face it, one glance at Cassis's devastatingly beautiful face would have any girl—and many guys—writhing in their underwear. I push my thighs together, and another fleeting smile touches Cassis's mouth, as if he is well aware of where my thoughts strayed to.

More likely he just assumes everything is about him.

I put down my drink and sit, cringing as the blood from my cut arm drips onto the polished leather. "If you're going to add the cleaning to my debt, can I have a bigger towel or something to keep down the damage?"

Cassis frowns, his brow creasing in a way that instantly transforms his face from mischief to intensity. Rising, he disappears into an adjacent room, returning a few moments later with a leather bag that looks like something the doctor on *Little House on the Prairie* carried around.

Setting the bag on the coffee table, Cassis pulls out a leather case with medical tools and a large syringe, the latter wrapped in the sterile blister pack that is most definitely from the modern century. A small vial follows, Cassis expertly piercing the top with a hypodermic needle and injecting a bit of air into the vial before drawing up a clear liquid. Turning the syringe needle up, Cassis depresses the plunger until a bead of moisture crowns the sharp tip and shines menacingly against the recess lights. "Give me your hand."

"When pigs fly." I'm on my feet before the words are out of my mouth, putting a good two paces of distance between us. "If you think I'm letting you inject me with anything, think again."

Cassis tosses me the vial he just drew from. "It's lidocaine."

"You fancy yourself some kind of doctor?" I ask.

That amused smile cuts across his sensuous mouth again. "I have a medical degree or five."

"Playing hospital in nursery school doesn't count." Cassis looks barely thirty—though I know looks have nothing to do with it when it comes to immortals. "I don't care what label you put on your drugs, you aren't injecting me with anything."

"As you wish." Cassis depresses the plunger on the syringe, letting all the clear liquid squirt into the air. "Would you prefer I hand you the tweezers and you can pull the shards out yourself? I hear it can be pleasant, feeling each tiny little piece cut the flesh just a bit deeper as it moves."

Bile rises up my throat, but just to prove to him that I can, I walk over and grab a pair of bent grippy things from his leather torture collection. Then I take one look at my hand, watch the room spin, and toss the damn things back on the table—or try to, the round grips tangling on my suddenly clumsy fingers.

Powerful hands brace my back and legs before I can fall, lifting me easily onto the couch. Cassis crouches beside me. His cologne smells of sin and spice, and there's a fresh scent of shampoo wafting from his hair. Even though he holds himself very still, I can feel the tension roaring inside his body, as if beneath the easy motions and cocky jests, he's fighting against himself.

"Do you really not understand what would happen if you walked through Dusk like this?" Cassis asks, his gaze gripping mine, his impossibly broad shoulders filling my vision. The intensity of his deep-chocolate eyes now tempers that playboy image he gave off down in the club. "Do you understand who I am?" Cassis's voice is low. "What am I?"

"A vampire, right?" I snort lightly. "Fae, vampires, witches. I got it."

Cassis doesn't smile back. "You have no understanding of what that means, though, do you?" he says, rubbing his hand over his face. "Hell take me."

15

Cassis

Cassis was going to disembowel Ellis. What was the idiot thinking, sending Samantha to Dusk to say she was a witch, even as a joke? The girl had to be a demi, with no concept of the danger she was in coming here—and she wasn't exactly inconspicuous, that small gorgeous body packing a fire-filled soul that filled his entire club the moment she'd entered. Samantha had woken something inside Cassis, which he didn't think was possible anymore. Not after Sienna.

Curiosity. That was all Cassis was feeling. His compulsion failed on Samantha, and that alone was fascinating. That, and the naïveté.

"How long have you known about the other species?" he asked, settling beside Sam on the couch. Pulling a throw pillow onto his lap, he pulled the girl's injured hand gently atop it, a zing of possessive energy shooting through him as his skin brushed hers. She was tense. Hurt and scared, but scared of all the wrong things.

"Ten days." She swallowed.

Cassis snorted. "Let me guess, the only full vampires you met until today were Academy instructors?"

Sam nodded, fine-boned face pale as he inspected her cuts.

"Ellis is one sick bastard," he muttered, willing to bet his fangs that the bastard was behind this little visit. Gripping Sam's hand firmly enough to stabilize it, Cassis used the tweezers to pluck the first small shard of glass free. Bloody hell, but it felt good to see Sam's small shoulders relax a fraction as she realized it didn't hurt as badly as she clearly feared. It would have hurt even less if she'd allowed Cassis to numb it, but he respected the caution.

He just wished it was aimed in the right direction.

"Word of advice—don't bleed in front of vampires you don't know. It's like walking into a club in nothing but a thong and expecting not to be propositioned." Cassis weighed Sam with his gaze and, deciding that she was unlikely to pass out if he stood her up, put a hand in the small of her back. The couple of shards were out, and he wanted to run some water over that hand to get a better look at the damage.

He wouldn't mind running some water over himself while he was at it. Some very, very cold water.

"Fine, I'll bite," said Sam, the corners of Cassis's mouth twitching at her choice of words, even as the way her body accepted his support made his chest tighten. "If I'm all that appetizing to vampires, how are you here not drinking me dry?"

"This isn't the thirteenth century, Samantha. Killing has consequences." He opened the door to the bathroom, the gleaming white tile complementing the matte gold faucet handles that Cassis had had the designer shape like wolf heads in honor of Ellis and Asher. That way, he could wring their necks each time he turned the water on. "Also, taking another's blood without permission is impolite."

Samantha laughed, the musical sound making Cassis's chest— and other parts—clench uncomfortably. If Ellis had been a bastard to send the girl his way, then Cassis was no better now, allowing her to lean into him. To think that he could be trusted.

Enough.

Moving quickly enough to leave the girl gasping, Cassis put both his hands on the edge of the sink, trapping her in the circle of his arms. Sam swallowed as he loomed over her, piercing her with a look that sent most full vampires to their knees.

Cassis could hear Sam's pulse quicken, smell the scent of sudden, overdue fear that spilled into her blood—and all the time, her face never shifted from that fiery stubbornness that seemed to be her signature look. Reaching to Sam's neck, he ran the tip of his blunt nail across the soft spot that twitched with every beat of her heart.

"Blood is powerful," he said, the shiver running through Sam's body confirming the darkness in his voice. "One mouthful and I will know your secrets, Samantha. I will taste your very life. Don't mistake my control for safety. Not with me. Not with any of my kind. Do you understand?"

"Yeah." She pushed his hand away, breaking eye contact with too great an ease. "Thank you for, err, not drinking my blood and secrets there, Dracula. I'll be sure to stock up on garlic and holy water for the next time I see you. And a cross. Better safe than sorry, right?"

Bloody hell, she was incorrigible. Cassis shook his head, the grin he'd been really, *really* trying to hide escaping onto his face. How long had it been since a female could go toe to toe with him? To rouse a deep protective instinct? "I like garlic, holy water most often comes from the tap, and I've known more than one vampire to take up the cloth. What the bloody hell are the geniuses at the Academy teaching you?"

"How to fall on my ass, mostly."

"You are a lost cause, Samantha." Cassis shook his head. Rebellious red-streaked hair, a stubborn mouth, eyes alight with all the energy of the world despite everything that had just happened to her. And beyond that, if he looked closely enough, a flicker of loneliness. And far too much bravery. Any other nonvampire would never have set foot into Dusk. For reasons he couldn't begin to fathom, he ached to brush Sam's face, to feel her smooth creamy skin. Reaching behind her, and squashing that ache with a firm shove, Cassis turned on the faucet instead and nudged her hand under the running water.

The scent of her blood rose into the air at once, the pink-tinged water sparking like wine, down to the tiny little bubbles. For all the self-control Cassis usually possessed—he hadn't been joking about the medical degrees, though those were back from a time he'd given a damn—he turned his face away. When he finally peered down to examine Sam's palm, his whole body froze at the star-shaped scar looking back at him.

For the second time in his life, Cassis had been sucker punched by a witch.

1 6

Sam

"**W**hat is that?" Cassis demands, a growl rising through his chest. My head spins in an effort to work out what the hell just happened, and it takes several moments and more of his growling to work out that the vampire is talking about the puckered star-shaped scar over my palm. Courtesy of one of my foster mothers, who thought a heated paperweight would make just the right discipline tool for a wayward brat.

I yank my hand away. "Nothing."

Everything around Cassis suddenly chills to ice. "Don't lie to me."

My heart stutters, a healthy wave of fear suddenly rushing through my veins. I back away, sticking my hand into my pocket, a move that's become instinct by now. A way to avoid the conversation I've had for years. *I was playing near the radiator at home. My mom told me to be careful so many times. But I was silly. I touched a hot handle. Yes, it's star shaped. Burned my palm. I should have listened to Mom. I'm very sorry.*

"Tell me!" Cassis's voice thunders through the apartment with the wrath of a storm, echoing off the white tile.

"A burn," I snap back at him. "From childhood. I grabbed a hot knob on a heater at our apartment."

His eyes darken, the sudden turn to revulsion—to hatred—in their black depths making me gasp for breath. "You are lying to me, witch."

I shove him away, my palms hitting a chest as hard and immobile as Ellis's. "Fuck off, Cassis. I don't owe you an explanation."

"No?" Cassis's hand, which so gently tended my cuts minutes ago, wraps itself in my hair. He yanks my head up and to the side, his beautiful face full of such menace that it's all I can do to bite back a scream. "You shouldn't have come," he growls, his elongated canines flashing in the florescent light.

And then I do scream. In terror and then in pain as Cassis's teeth sink into the soft spot of my neck. All of Ellis's lessons flee from me as I flail against Cassis's unyielding hold, my fist and legs striking whatever they can find as the world swims around me. Before going dark.

I COME AWAKE to a set of strong hands cradling me against a muscular chest, Cassis's smooth, heady musk washing through my senses. His polished piano sits silently in my line of sight. My neck is sore, and I reach up to finger a piece of gauze covering the side of it. Then the memories return, and I fling myself off the couch with the speed of a raging bull. Or try to. I actually end up stumbling off, only to be caught by Cassis's hands before my face hits the ground.

Without needing to be told to get the hell away from me, he deposits me on the couch and steps away, the brooding guilt on his face making his jaw clench.

"What. The hell. Happened?" My words come in pants, my hands curling into fists.

"I bit you." Another tic twitches along Cassis's jaw, and he steps away to pour two glasses of whiskey, placing one on the low table beside me. "I shouldn't have done that."

I let out a shaking breath. Insane. The vampire is fucking insane.

Or maybe I'm the insane one, having followed Ellis's advice to come here. "Right. Very…impolite." I look at the door, wondering if my legs will support me if I try to stand. How much blood did I lose? My hand tightens on the glass, a very different thought rushing through me. "Am I… Did you…"

"You are still a witch, Samantha. You'd know if you were turned, trust me. For one thing, it requires dying." The hint of amusement in Cassis's tone dies as quickly as it flared. "You passed out from the shock, not blood loss. I took only a mouthful. Enough to know you're an innocent in all this."

I rub my palm, seeing Cassis's muscles go rigid at the sight of the scar.

"All what?"

He shakes his head. "It doesn't matter. Back when there were more of your kind around, a witch and I had a bit of a disagreement. Your scar reminded me of something she did, but that something had nothing to do with a heated paperweight." Cassis's nostrils flare at that, and I remember him mentioning something about blood holding information.

"Do you know all of my life now?" I cross my arms over my chest, feeling naked.

Putting down his drink, Cassis crouches beside me. "No, Samantha. I took one mouthful, and with it whatever emotions and memories coursed through it at the time. Given that we'd been discussing the burn, I know how you got it, but not much more than that." He lowers his head, his broad shoulders falling in apology beneath the expensive suit. "I…apologize."

I've had people hurt me plenty. Apologize for it? That's a first. Which is fairly messed up as far as life is concerned. I'm not sure what to make of any of this, beyond the fact that Ellis set me up and I hate him.

"Let's get back to the *all this* you so skillfully brushed past," I say, shooting him a hard look. If Cassis is actually half as contrite as he's letting on, he owes me. "How do you know Ellis, and what does my scar have to do with anything?"

Cassis pinches the bridge of his nose and looks at me from under those dark lashes. "Let's agree that I owe you a favor."

I smile like a fox. "Yes, let's. And I'm collecting. Talk."

"You have a favor from me, and you want to use it on a bit of four-hundred-year-old gossip?" Cassis cocks a brow, but I can see there's strain behind it.

"Yep," I say without hesitation. Another thing I've learned in foster care is that you never *ever* take a promise of later payment. A quarter now is worth more than a dollar never.

Cassis finishes his whiskey in a single gulp and gets to his feet. Setting the empty glass on the piano top, he takes off the black Versace and undoes the black-diamond cuff links. The red shirt is barely wrinkled, and for an idiotic second, I wonder if the vampire does his own ironing. The thought of Cassis, bare to the waist beside an ironing board, his muscles shifting as he gets his things together, is as delicious as it's absurd.

Then Cassis reaches around himself to pull the shirt off, and all the images swimming in my head shatter in an instant.

"What the hell do you think you're doing?" I demand, wobbling slightly as I jump to my feet and maneuver to get the couch between us.

"I'm answering your question," Cassis answers calmly. "As you requested."

A tug of fabric and the male is bare to the waist, the smooth, square muscles of his abdomen stacked like a wall of perfectly cut stones. Taut pale skin stretches over a broad, muscled chest, the warm lighting sculpting the shadows into an artistic perfection that sends a wave of heat to my cheeks. And to other places.

Instead of preening, however—which, let's be honest, he has every right to be doing with that body—Cassis gives his empty glass a mournful look and turns his back to me, his hands bracing against the piano.

My breath halts, and I'm moving toward Cassis before I can think through the wisdom of it. Moving toward the star-shaped burn mark right there over his shoulder blade, the puckered skin thick and stark. When I brush the tip of my finger over his skin,

Cassis flinches as if struck, his grip on the piano blanching his knuckles. But he holds still anyway, even with the fine tremor that rushes through his body.

"Who did this?" I ask.

"A witch named Sienna." Cassis steps away, turning to face me. "Vampires, fae, and witches were at each other's throats at the time. Much like now, but without the pretend honey layer of civility. That was before Talonswood became neutral ground too. Sienna and I were natural enemies, but…" He shrugs one powerful shoulder. "I fell in love. More than that, I thought I was mating, that Sienna had a piece of my soul."

Cassis gives me a humorless smile and goes to refill his glass. "She had similar thoughts for that soul of mine. She tried to cut it out with a spell. Literally." He says nothing for a few moments as he takes another drink before pulling his shirt back on. "Vampires don't usually scar —or, more accurately, we do, but the marks fade in time. Sienna's work… Well. She put some effort in."

My heart clenches, and I reach toward the male, pulling back before making contact. No wonder he dislikes witches. And star-shaped scars. "What happened to Sienna?" I ask, curling my hand into a fist to keep from brushing his face. "Did you kill her?"

Cassis shakes his head. "We couldn't. But never underestimate the destructive power of humans. What four immortals couldn't accomplish, the Spanish Inquisition took care of with brutal efficiency."

"Four immortals?"

"That is not my story to tell. And you should be getting back to the Academy." Cassis reaches into his back pocket for a cell phone, the vulnerable male from a few moments ago gone behind the suave cockiness I met earlier. "I'm going to ask Reese to come get you."

"No!" I grab his wrist before he can punch in the number, and he freezes, slowly looking from my hand up to my face. My cheeks heat, and I pull away, my attention still on the phone. I don't know what Reese or the other cadre will do exactly if they catch me out of bounds, but I'm assuming it will hurt.

"There is no Uber here, Samantha."

"I'll get back on my own."

"Not an option."

"Like hell it's not."

"I forgot. You've been around here ten days. You know everything." A corner of his mouth twitches, taking the sting out of his words. "Reese or Ellis. Those are your options. Well, or Asher, but I highly, *highly* recommend you don't chose that one. Asher likes rules."

Before I can reply, the front door opens with a bang, revealing a blond predator whose gaze shoots daggers into Cassis. Holding a phone in his free hand, Ellis spares me half a glance, the hilt of an honest-to-God sword peeking over his shoulder and somehow looking completely right with his fitted jeans and black T-shirt. "Get your coat, Devinee."

I glare at Cassis, any kind feelings I'd had toward the male gone in a flash. "You already called him." The whole pretense of pulling out a phone was just a fucking show. Cassis shrugs without a shred of remorse. "I knew the bastard would be close by. Though I'd hoped not *this* close. Don't forget you still owe me for the tab, Samantha."

17

Sam

Ellis says nothing as he walks me down the stairs and through the club, the menace around him enough to keep the vampires snarling but giving way until we're at the door. As soon as we get into the cool outside night air, I twist toward him in a silent demand for an explanation. He was the one who set me up for this.

"Am I going to need tetanus shots thanks to you?" I ask.

He reaches for my neck and pulls off the bandage, his emotionless expression holding no hint of surprise as he examines the puncture marks. Yes, he *did* set me up, sending me over to Cassis, who he knew hated witches. Baiting the vampire into an attack. But why? My hand closes around the scar on my palm, and I wonder whether Ellis knew it was there. Whether that scar had anything to do with luring me into Cassis's lair.

Fingering the bite mark, I'm surprised to find that it no longer hurts. It seems vampire bites heal faster than normal wounds. Adding that to the list of absurd facts to keep track off, I return to glaring at Ellis. "Well?"

Instead of answering, he gestures at my outfit with a building storm in his eyes. "I told you to go talk to Cassis. I *didn't* tell you to go in looking like vamp bait."

I look down at my ruined lace cami, breasts straining out the top, and suddenly feel naked—and ridiculous. "I wasn't trying to look like—"

Ellis suddenly steps in close to me so I have to crane my neck back to hold his gaze. "You already smell delicious to them, Devinee. A sizzling steak after a two-week fast. Lust and hunger are nearly one and the same for vamps, so when you *look* appetizing too, it only intensifies the temptation."

"Fuck you, Ellis." I twist on him. "This whole male thing of 'dressed like that, you're asking for me to do whatever I want' excuse is as fucked up here as anywhere. So don't even start."

Instead of answering, the asshole turns and starts walking before I can say anything, his dark jeans and T-shirt disappearing quickly into the shadows, giving me no choice but to follow. "We will stay to the streets as long as we can, but we will have to go through the woods for a half mile at least. There is only one well-patrolled road to Academy grounds, and you are too fragile to deal with basic punishment."

"That isn't an answer to anything," I snap. "Why did you set me and Cassis up? Whatever information he learned about me, something tells me he won't be sending you a report."

"He doesn't need to," Ellis replies without bothering to look at me. "That fact that you're still alive provides me all the information I require."

"What's that supposed to mean?" I step in front of Ellis, though I have to nearly jog to get there. "And does it have anything to do with someone named Sienna?"

I see it then, a flash of pain in Ellis's eyes before he schools his expression to neutrality. But before I can press further, the air around the male bends, his body changing before my eyes until there's a snow-white wolf glaring at me with golden eyes instead. The wolf who I mistook for a dog in the mansion. Holy fucking shit.

I mean, I knew fae shifted and all, but knowing and seeing it happen aren't the same thing.

"Coward," I tell the animal, not sure whether Ellis's wolf form can actually understand human.

The wolf walks around me, and…

"What the hell?" I jump back as I realize he's lifted a leg to pee on my boot. Yeah. Lovely. Promising myself that one way or the other I'm going to make Ellis pay for all this, I turn off the road early and head into the woods just to be contrary. I half expect the wolf to get in my way, but the animal plainly has his own preferences and, raising his tail, happily trots into the dark brush and disappears from view.

After Newark, where bail bonds and strip club signs flashed at all hours, the utter dark silence of Talonswood is downright eerie. About ten minutes into my hike, I'm forced to conclude that I've just successfully cut off my nose to spite my face. Despite the moon and star-filled sky, which is the only reason I'm able to see at least the vague outlines of a trail, the forest is even darker than it was when I snuck through it to get to town. At the slower speed I'm walking, the extra half mile or so I've added to my route will easily add half an hour. I need to get my hands on a flashlight if I'm going to keep doing this.

That said, there is a majesty out here. The scents of soil, leaf, and pine are fresh and clean, and though the only forest noise I recognize is that of the owl hooting in the distance, I like the sense of quiet life around me. It's like being alone but not. Maybe Ellis's shift into wolf form was to give me these few extra minutes, a small peace offering after setting me up. "This does not make us even," I say aloud, though I know the asshole can't hear me. "Not by a long shot."

Two steps later, a body slams into me fast and hard, driving me into the ground.

Breath leaves me as I hit the uneven dirt and buck, twisting about like a worm trying to escape the earth beneath my attacker. Turning my head to get a gasp of breath, I find a thick, callused palm clapping over my mouth.

"Stay quiet if you want to live," Ellis purrs into my ear. My blood goes cold at the sound. "We aren't alone."

The instant I stop struggling, he lifts off me, jerking me to my feet by the back of my jacket with a strength far from human.

"What—"

Ellis claps his hand over my mouth again. "Quiet," he whispers into my ear, his words taking on a battlefield calm that is both soothing and terrifying. Gripping my upper arm, he half pulls, half drags me the base of a large oak, throwing me into dark brush at its base before spinning around. In the moonlight, I see a sword—a real-life gleaming sword—flashing in the male's hands just as someone pounces onto the patch of earth we stood on moments ago.

The man—no, not a man—a deformed kind of thing with a man's body and beast-like legs that bend in the wrong direction snarls as it twists around in a circle. Bright yellow eyes lock on me, saliva dripping from the thing's mouth onto his hairy chest. A were —a half-turned demi—it has to be.

Ellis's lithe body coils and strikes, smooth and fast as a whip. I've never seen him, never seen anyone, move like that before. So fast, it's slow. Smooth. Utterly controlled as he puts the creature down in a single blow that has me clamping my hands over my mouth to keep in bile.

The thing falls with a thud, but Ellis stays crouched, his sword out as he surveys the night and listens to those phantom sounds that mean nothing to me. Stopping with his attention on a pair of dark trees that look like any other lumps of shadow to me, Ellis lets out a low soft growl that sounds more animal than human.

"Didn't anyone tell you not to bring a knife to a gun fight?" A rough voice precedes a heavily armed man stepping out from the tree cluster. The laser sights of his handgun—pointed right at Ellis's chest—glow a florescent green. Though I can't work out the details of the man's appearance, his silhouette suggests he is not only armed for the apocalypse but is wearing body armor to boot.

What in the holy fucking hell?

"Where is the witch?" the man asks, his gun steady. At this range, he can't possibly miss.

"At the Academy," Ellis answers conversationally. "You should go ask after her."

"Cute," says the man and squeezes the trigger.

18

Sam

I gasp as a gun flashes, the discharge booming through the forest as a figure falls to his knees. A man's scream fills the night, and, despite myself, I rush toward the sound.

"Ellis!" I call, the name echoing through the woods.

Ellis. Ellis.

A hard hand grips the back of my jacket, jerking me around. Ellis's familiar golden eyes flash in the starlight.

"Goddamn it, Devinee," he snaps, but keeps hold on my jacket until my breath steadies. "I told you to stay back."

"But..." I blink. I saw the gun fire. Saw a man fall. Why—my racing thoughts come to a screeching halt as I take in the reality before me. A man on his knees, still in his Kevlar body armor, clutching a bleeding arm, his gun lying on the ground beside him... with his hand still attached to the weapon.

Holy. Fucking. Shit. Ellis sliced the man's hand clean off.

I clamp my hands over my mouth and back away to steady myself against a tree trunk while Ellis strips the man of his remaining weapons. Snatching something floppy looking off the man's vest, Ellis throws it into his lap. "I hope you know how to use your own tourniquet."

The man claws for the device, somehow managing to wrap it around his bleeding stump.

"Word of advice, hunter. Don't bring a gun to a sword fight," Ellis calls over his shoulder, his sights now set on me. Stopping a short step away, he weighs me with a kind of gaze that misses nothing, from my weak knees to the way my fingers dig into the bark. "I did tell you to stay to the streets until the final road."

I stare blankly. What difference would it have made? Not to mention that I just strolled through these woods to get to the town to begin with. As Ellis made sure I would do.

He seems to follow my train of thought, because he shakes his head. "I followed you on your way out, Devinee. Watched every step you took from my wolf form." His hand extends, taking hold of my chin before I can turn away, the steady power of his touch gripping me like a lifeline. "I wouldn't have let you go into the woods if I hadn't been certain I could protect you."

I swallow numbly, his words forcing their way through my thick cotton-swaddled mind. The way he said *let* me go, as if my actions are in any way his choice. The cocky assumptions of his own abilities. And yet—yet he did win the fight without so much as breathing harder. How can words that I want to punch him for give me a measure of comfort all at the same time?

"Look at me, Devinee." Crouching in front of me, Ellis touches my cheek with a gentleness that makes the breath freeze in my lungs. His tone softens, the stunning change sending a flood of warmth through me no matter how hard I fight against it. I didn't know he was capable of softness. "Are you hurt?"

Me? "I wasn't the one who was shot at." I swallow. The hunter had been so damn close. "How did he miss?"

"He didn't. The bullet grazed me a bit." Ellis shrugs one shoulder, his controlled expression showing no sign of the pain that I know must grip him. "I'm not human. I'll heal."

"But..." My words falter, and I fight down the instinct to reach out to the male. Hardened and deadly as he is, I don't think he'd let me touch him even if we liked each other. Which we don't.

Despite his own admonishment, Ellis picks up the discarded handgun and gives it to me grip first. "I'm going to drop this scum into one of the were cages." His voice is calm and steady, an anchor amidst chaos. A trained voice. "I want you to wait here. Can you do that?"

I feel the male's absence the moment he dissolves silently into the forest, my mind immediately replaying the night's events. The were. The hunter. How easily, how efficiently, Ellis killed. What would have happened if he hadn't been here.

Night sounds move in, each one of them terrifying now instead of soothing. Every rustle in the undergrowth, every snapping twig and soft hoot, something dark moving closer and closer and closer...

I'm still exactly where Ellis left me when he returns, my muscles so tight, they've started to ache. Plucking the weapon gently out of my shaking hands, he gives it a condescending look before tucking it into his waistband. "The problem with guns is that they make you think you're invincible. There are no shortcuts to training." He touches my shoulder. "Come, Devinee. I'll need to report the hunter to Asher so he can have the woods swept clean. It should have been done before liberty, as everyone knows how cadets get."

I have nothing to say. That distant owl hoots again, and the storm inside my mind howls in answer. Without thinking of what I'm doing, I step away from Ellis. From the Academy. From this place where dead bodies and severed limbs are just a nuisance to be dealt with, where vampires sip my blood to learn my secrets. Where Ellis tries to kill me and save me at even intervals, punctuated by periods of cool torment. "I want out," I say quietly. Then louder: "I don't have magic, and I'm done. I want out."

"It doesn't work that way, Samantha," Ellis says, wiping his sword with a handful of dried leaves before sheathing it down his back. "You don't leave Talonswood until Talonswood says you do."

"Yes, I've watched enough prison movies to know the rules. Been in a few as well."

"This isn't some human prison," Ellis snaps at me in a thick brogue, his patience cracking with a force I haven't seen before. "You have to have figured that out by now. You would never make it out of these woods alive today. And if you did—let's say by some miracle of hell itself you ran away from me now and found a way off the island—you would be hunted until the end of your life. By the Council and by the hunters. Trapped on both sides."

"And if I finish your little charade?" I demand. "You want to tell me that things are going to be rosy and happy? Or you think I'm too smart to have missed all the problems, but just dumb enough to believe they would go away the moment I left?"

"When—if—you finish Talonswood, you will at least be sanctioned by the Council." He stops, the sculpted lines of his face tight as he weighs his words with a miser's scale. "You aren't human. There are some consequences that come with having magic course through your veins."

"There is no magic coursing through anything!" I snap back at him. "Tell me why. Why Talonswood is so insistent on—"

"You know why. Talonswood Reform exists because while fae mating with fae produces nice little fae pups, and vampires turn adults, we can't stop cocks from going into pussies all over the world. Hence, demis. Mostly human, but partly not. So we've a whole crop of these hybrids who are all faster, or heal quickly, or can influence others to do their bidding with their gaze—and they don't even know it. They think they're that great, that powerful all by themselves. And given the nature of most of these couplings, they don't usually have a great family life. So this is the solution. The reform school and jail that not everyone comes out of alive. Because we can't afford to have a few idiots start a new war."

"I'm not a fucking demi."

"You may as well be," Ellis snaps. "Did you listen to what I just said? Beside your actual DNA, I just described *you*, Devinee. A creature who doesn't know what her own magic is capable of. Doesn't even know when she's using it. How is it that you can't run two miles without tripping over your own feet, but somehow climbing into windows to steal was never an issue? How did you go so long without ever getting caught? You. Don't. Know. Wars have been started over lesser things than witch magic. So yes, no one is letting you go any time soon."

Talonswood would rather see me dead than see me run. And no one would so much as lift a hand to care. My back hits a tree trunk, and I realize with a start that I've been moving all this time, Ellis keeping pace with me.

"The things in the woods?" I ask, already knowing the answer, but needing Ellis to confirm it anyway.

"Demis gone wrong. Some are not human enough to exist in society, so they live here. They don't usually come this close to civilization, but I have a feeling our hunter friend drove it out this way to flush out anyone he might take down. There's always an idiot now and then who wants to try his hand against a creature. Given how many idiots try to climb Everest, I guess I should be surprised there aren't more of these loners… Devinee. Samantha!"

I've stopped listening, my body starting to shake as I sink to the ground.

After a pause and then a muffled curse, Ellis pulls me against him. The warmth of his large body wraps around mine. "I have you," he says softly, his concern-laden voice nearly comical after all the ways he's tormented me the past weeks. Before I can answer, he slides one hand beneath my knees and lifts me easily against his chest, his hands tightening around me when I start to protest. "Enough adventure for one night, witch," he informs me flatly, his breath rustling my hair. "I'm taking over for the rest of it. You can be back to your spitfire self first thing in the morning."

19

Sam

*E*llis somehow gets us back to campus unnoticed and then deposits me in his room while he changes and goes out to speak with Asher. I wait for the cadre's wrath to descend upon me for all of a quarter hour before falling asleep in the male's twin bed. When I wake again, Ellis is back in the room, sleeping on the floor —an arrangement that should make me uncomfortable given that he's blocking the exit, but finds me too exhausted to care.

By the time I finally wake up for the day—having slept through half of my second liberty day—the sun is high up in the sky and the room is empty once more. I take a moment to notice what I didn't last night—the bone-spare neatness of the small white-walled space, no clothes or books on any surface, one neatly folded towel on the corner of the desk. Either Ellis came here expecting not to stay long, or he simply has no personal items. Part of me suspects the latter.

By the following morning, however, my life at Talonswood Reform somehow falls back into its normal cadence, as if the night out in the club and woods had never happened. If anything, in fact,

Ellis comes at me with even less mercy during morning training and speaks to me equally little at all other times.

What Ellis lacks in words, however, the rest of the Academy makes up for in a buzz of conversation. Someone named Count Victor is coming to inspect the Academy, and apparently, there's nothing more fitting with which to welcome a member of the Council than a full-on ball. The occasion is grand enough that even Bernadette condescends to talk to me, needing to know which of the three dresses she ordered best showcases her perfect body.

"Why is everyone so wound up around Victor anyway?" I ask, watching the dress unboxing, with slinky green, red, and silver garments spilling like flower vomit over Bernadette's bed.

"Seriously?" She gives me a look designed to grind cockroaches into the floor. "Victor is one of the most powerful vampires alive. His clan rules Romania and beyond. This little visit might officially be to inspect the Academy, but all the vamps know Victor is looking for fresh strong blood to join his clan."

I don't bother pointing out that a powerful vampire seeking to expand his clan is unlikely to pick from a group of demi delinquents. If Bernadette and her cohort want to parade around like peacocks, that's their prerogative. Me, I'm staying right here and sleeping.

"You can't," says Bernadette, making me realize that I said the last part out loud. "The ball is compulsory." Her glossed lips quirk into a self-satisfied smile, green eyes sparkling with whatever insult she's about to deliver. "Though being the only one to show up wearing a school uniform might not provide you with the same experience. Too bad there are no witches to fund your expenses, eh?"

Ah, yes. The trusts. I was wondering where my classmates were getting funds for everything from designer clothing to contraband alcohol for several weeks before discovering that both vampires and fae have trust funds set up to issue allowances to the demis of their species. Even a bad investment held for a few hundred years yields good results—so, given the immortals' life span, neither species is exactly lacking for money.

A knock at the door saves me from having to answer. For a moment, I just frown at the large box on the floor with my name on it—right beneath an embossed Versace label. "What the hell?" I say, echoing Bernadette's similar question as I open the lid to reveal a skintight off-the-shoulder red sheath, with matching satin stilettos and a diamond collar necklace. By the sudden darkening of Bernadette's stare, the little sparkly things studding the shoes are as real as the larger ones in the jewelry.

I shake my head. There's no note, but there is one male I know who likes the brand.

"Looks like I'll be attending without a plaid skirt after all," I tell her sweetly as she turns from me with a huff.

I WALK across the lamplit green alone, shivering lightly in the cool pine-scented air, carrying the ridiculous studded heels in one hand. Better save my feet for when it counts. The west castle, which I've never been in before, is lit brilliantly from within, buzzing with the sounds of music and colliding voices. My stomach trembles with nerves, and I press a hand over it, feeling the rich red fabric slip under my fingers.

When I walk into the entrance hall, a somber stone affair with one iron chandelier overhead, a human waiter wearing white gloves bows immediately, giving me instructions on how to get myself from the front door all the way to another door about five steps away. I pause by a ten-foot gold-framed mirror to put on the heels, taking a second to make sure there's no lipstick on my chin or food in my teeth.

I look like a stranger. The red dress skims over my body, showing curves that I've only ever tried to hide. A long slit reaches up my right thigh—which I've left bare, in spite of the nude hose Cassis put in the box—and the dress's bodice hugs my breasts tightly, making them swell from the top in a way that makes me feel incredibly exposed. My hair falls in loose waves to my shoulders, and together with the red lipstick and mascara I "borrowed" from Bernadette, I look nothing like Sam of Newark.

I take a deep breath. Then walk carefully through the arched doorway into the ballroom—and straight into a legit fairy tale. I swallow a gasp, feeling a silly smile spread across my face. A two-story-high vaulted ceiling painted into a gold-kissed sunset sky, shining marble columns, twinkling lights strung between them like stars, a polished hardwood floor that gleams nearly as much as the crystal champagne flutes in people's hands.

On a dais to the right, a quartet of violins fills the space with the most soul-shattering sounds I've ever heard. I close my eyes for a moment, just listening, letting peace wash over me, calming the jumping nerves in my stomach.

Distantly, I notice voices beginning to fall away, notice a heavy weight falling over the room. I open my eyes in confusion. All around me, in a wave spreading through the ballroom, faces have turned toward me, dances paused midstep, conversations midsentence.

Some eyes are widened in surprise, some in confusion as they try to place who I am—but most of the cadets wear some version of the same expression. Hatred, mixed with jealousy, as they take in my outfit piece by piece. And my hips and breasts, as if they didn't know I had them. I feel naked under their hot-eyed inspection, and I can tell immediately that I've crossed some line, done something I shouldn't have. I feel a heavy gaze to my left and turn to find Ellis in a black tuxedo, golden eyes hard on my body, mouth twisted in disapproval. His pale hair is tucked neatly behind his ears tonight, brushing his collar.

Finally, right as I'm about to flee the room for good, furious at the tears pressing against the backs of my eyes, the conversations and dancing haltingly pick back up, decorum taking over once more. I start looking for a corner to hide in, but a cool palm slides over my lower back, and I turn to find a tall dark-haired vampire in a tight-fitting Versace tuxedo by my side. If I thought Cassis's suit at Dusk was spectacular, this one is cut to show off his broad shoulders and taut waist with a designer's perfection. I notice the red handkerchief in his pocket, the exact same shade as my dress—and the male's small, satisfied smile as I do.

"Ignore them, Samantha," he murmurs. "You look positively sinful."

"What are you doing here?" I ask, trying to also ignore the mix of heat and indignation that his closeness sends through me. The gorgeous bastard all but put a claiming tag on me with that little move, and I hate how much I like it. Plus, from the piercing looks still coming my way, I have a feeling that standing here with him is doing nothing to help my cause. Sex and power drip off him as clearly as a scent, drawing every demivamp eye in the room, female and male.

"I didn't think you ever stepped foot on Academy grounds," I say, trying to keep my words from shaking.

"Not when there isn't a party." Cassis takes a drink from the tray of a passing waitress without either missing a step—or caring who the whiskey's intended recipient was. Stepping within arm's reach, he raises his glass, an approving smile tugging his lips. "Here's to my estimation of a female's figure. I am pleased to see the skill hasn't left me."

The heat in my cheeks pulses. "You shouldn't have." He *really* shouldn't have.

"But you are glad I did," Cassis purrs, his perfectly coiffed dark hair and smoothly angled face those of a perfectly delicious playboy. As if the male who trembled as he showed me the scar on his back never existed. Cassis lifts both brows at me. "So, when did you figure it out?"

"When I saw the too-low neckline and utterly absent back, Cassis." I bite my lip. Snark aside, the gown is the most beautiful piece of clothing I've ever worn, much less owned. "I—thank you."

"Ah, so the witch does have those words in her vocabulary." The corner of his mouth twitches in a smile, and he deposits his empty glass on an approaching waiter's tray. Slipping the man a hundred dollar bill, Cassis plucks the two lone drinks from the same tray, handing one of the flutes to me.

Savoring the sweet, berry aroma, I curse under my breath. Cassis liquor. There was nothing accidental about this waiter's approach. The refreshments had been ordered before Cassis even started walking over to me.

I toast him the way he raised his glass to me and keep our gazes locked as I drink. I'll be damned if I give him the satisfaction of knowing he surprised me again. As the warm sip slides down my throat, I let my attention brush the eight-foot-diameter candlelit chandelier swaying from the top ceiling beam. The flickering candlelight reflects off the tall windows, which have the curtains pulled back to display the star-filled sky beyond. Making a full circle back, my attention rests on the violin quartet, the musicians now exchanging solemn notes as they tune their instruments.

"Where do you think the Academy found a quartet…suitable to be playing here?" I ask.

"They are vampires," Cassis says simply in answer to my unasked question, snatching a chocolate truffle from a passing waitress. Given the woman's surprised squawk, I expect her to smack his wrist for the offense, but seeing who just stole her order, she smiles instead. Of course she does.

"Is she a vamp too?" I ask.

"Not at all. We do employ humans with proper discretion." Cassis smiles at me, mischief written all over his eyes. "And just in case the discretion alone doesn't work, there are always other ways of persuasion."

"Compulsion," I say flatly.

"That and a lot of money," Cassis grins, allowing his canines to elongate slightly in a way that sends heat spiraling through me—and then shame that I somehow find murder weapons sexy. "They must have taught you something about compulsion in this great place they tell me is a school. Compulsion works much better when you suggest your mark do something they already would like to be doing."

"Is that how vamps make themselves feel good about compelling girls into their beds?" I ask, my drink suddenly tasting sour. "'She wanted it, otherwise my compulsion wouldn't have worked.'"

"I wouldn't know," Cassis answers, stepping close enough to me that I smell his spicy perfume, his powerful body spilling like liquid night through my space. Reaching out with his finger, Cassis traces a blunt, neatly trimmed nail along my jaw, and I feel myself dampening from the unspoken suggestion alone. The tip of his tongue flickers over his teeth, and he brings his lips so close to my ear that his breath tickles my skin. "I've never had a female not wanting to bed me."

"Cassis." Ellis's hard voice breaks between us as the male strides over with Asher, Reese following warily a few steps behind. Reese's eyes flick to me for a moment before settling somewhere in the air above Cassis's head. In a black suit with his dark hair slicked into a tight bun, hands clasped behind his back, he looks like a very dangerous, very expensive bodyguard. "Have you paid your respects to Count Victor yet? I think there might be a ring to be kissed or something similarly enticing."

"Oh, I've plenty of enticing ideas," Cassis says, dropping one hand casually on my hip while Ellis crosses his arms over his chest. "Few of them involving Victor, though."

The air between the males seems to thicken.

Exchanging a quick glance with Asher, Reese steps forward. The kind of step that would send mere mortals crawling under the closest bed. "Is there a problem, gentlemen?"

"Many," Cassis assures him.

"No, *sir*," Ellis says with no more respect in his tone than Cassis had a moment earlier.

I clear my throat, stepping forward with a shit-eating grin instead of running away like a smart person. "Can one of you tell me more about this Victor?" I ask, redirecting the males' attention with the time-honored power of annoying questions. "All I know is that he's a Council member and a powerful figure in, err, Romania."

A small smile of approval flickers over Reese's lips, which makes his severe face soften for a moment—and become far, far too beautiful. My knees soften right along with it, no matter how much I fight it.

"You are correct on both counts, Samantha. But one of the reasons Victor's presence in Talonswood is unusual is because his clan has always advocated for separation of the species." Reese turns slightly to watch a tall man, who I presume to be the count in question, making his rounds about the room. "He led the vampire forces during the fae-vamp wars. Though he was a great deal scruffier back then."

Tall and dark haired, Victor looks like he'd be in his midforties as a human and as fit as Cassis and the others. His pinstripe suit is slightly out of place amidst a sea of tuxedoes, but somehow, it makes the vampire look only more predatory. That and the way all the vampires he passes drop their gazes to the ground and go so far as to drop to their knees to extend Victor champagne and strawberries, which the male ignores as thoroughly as the kneeling demis. Victor's eyes survey the ball with battlefield precision, and I know the exact moment they land on me.

A chill tickles my neck, my hand inexplicably desperate to rub my throat. I do.

As one, Cassis and Ellis step toward the bar, as if suddenly craving a drink and coincidentally breaking the direct line of sight between Victor and me. The moment they do, my hand falls away from my throat, my muddled mind blinking away the confusion.

A test. The count tried to compel me from *across the room*, and it worked.

2 0

Sam

My breath quickens, and I clench my hands, my palms clammy.

"Look at me, Samantha," Reese orders softly, drawing all my attention to his face. Up close, his blue eyes are far from flat or expressionless—they swirl with thought and calculation, as if he's taking in every bit of information in the room all at once, and parsing out which he needs to pay attention to. "Take a deep breath."

The pupils of his eyes darken in that way I've come to associate with compulsion, and I step back away from him, doing the very opposite. "What the hell is it with you all?" I demand, before I realize who I'm talking to. My face pales. I've seen Reese discipline cadets for far less. "I'm sorry, sir."

Reese frowns, but seems more surprised than angry. "I will accept your apology if you accept mine," he says, that politeness slamming down like a wall between us. "But if I might ask, is there anyone else whose compulsion doesn't affect you? Plainly, Victor's did."

I frown. "Cassis. He tried once or twice. I think that's why he finds me…intriguing."

"Indeed," says Reese in that unreadable British accent of his.

"Your attention, please." Victor's rich baritone rolls through the ballroom, followed by the sound of a decorative knife clinking against crystal. "If I might borrow your ears for a few words."

The room quiets, the quartet toning down their music in perfect smoothness until there's just a hint of sound to provide ambiance to Victor's words.

"As many of you know, I've had quite a few centuries under my belt," Victor starts. "I was here when Talonswood Reform Academy was first established on the island. And to be honest, I did not think for a second that it would work. The Talonswood Island—so named for its forest and gateway to the Talon kingdom—is remarkable enough for being a neutral ground for all species, but could it be expected to support a whole academy? Blood-sworn enemies living and learning beneath the same roof? The idea was absolutely ludicrous. But yet here you are. Thriving. Bonding. Growing stronger together. It is an honor and a privilege to be standing here with you, seeing what you have built."

Victor pauses, his dark eyes swinging to me. "In fact, I understand this is the first year that Talonswood Reform is truly home to all three creature species. Please join me in a round of applause for the newest student, Samantha Devinee, a true witch, and Dean Javin, under whose unwavering leadership this fine institution thrives. *Noroc!*"

"*Noroc!*" The words echo throughout the room, the band striking up again as the guests politely empty their glasses. I'm fairly certain the mention of the absentee dean was a jab, but why mention me?

I answer my own question a moment later as Victor and Quinn walk directly toward me, Quinn all but prostrating himself before the older vampire. The cold kiss of Victor's gaze sends icicles down my spine as he and Quinn stop beside me.

"Count Victor," Quinn says with a bow, never looking Victor in the eye. "Allow me to introduce our newest student, Samantha Devinee."

"Good evening." Refusing to be intimidated, I keep my head raised and shoulders back as I extend my hand to the vampire.

Taking my hand gently between his fingers, Victor brings it to his mouth and brushes chilled lips over my knuckles. Up close, his power is even more overwhelming, the fine lines around his eyes and mouth betraying his more than a thousand years of age—and only serving to make him more distinguished. Even his scent seems intentional, as rich and heady as a fine aged red wine. "It is enchanting to make your acquaintance, my dear," he says. "Might you do me the honor of this dance?"

I can hear the music already swaying into a fox-trot, the notes singing to me in a way my feet have no chance of keeping up with. "I'm afraid I don't know how, Your…errr, Grace."

Victor laughs politely. "Your Excellence would do for a count, but such forms of address are largely out of style nowadays." Something about his tone says that, despite his words, this modern decline in etiquette makes him less than happy. "As for the dance, I believe I know the steps well enough to guide you through them if you would allow it."

I wonder if he means to compel me through the dance, but there isn't a way of asking that without creating a scene, especially since I'm already feeling his hand on my back, nudging me to the dance floor. Damn. The acoustics here are even better than on the sidelines. Of all the places the count could have chosen, the heart of music is the one place that gives me courage.

When I was a kid, some of the families' real children would take music lessons, and while I would never be permitted to do the same —who'd want to spend sixty dollars an hour to teach some foster brat piano?—they generally allowed me to watch. Discovering how the music was put together, understanding its language, it was like discovering fire on a cold dark night.

"The steps are simple," Victor assures me, his body swaying with the four-count beat. "It is very much like walking, but if you will allow me to take the lead, I think you'll find yourself enjoying it so much more." With the next beat, he steps through me, our bodies colliding in an odd way that's perfectly formal yet invasive.

"Have you discovered your powers yet, Ms. Devinee?" Victor asks casually, taking us into a turn that only an experienced dancer could pull off with a novice, the room spinning around us in streaks of candlelight.

"To tell you the truth, Your Excellence, I don't think I have any power at all. What of you? Is there something special about your skills? Can you turn into a bat, perhaps?"

"Human fables, my dear. It is the fae who shift into furry little creatures, not us." Victor spins us again, this time twirling so quickly that I get dizzy well before we stop, the count lifting me off my feet to keep me from falling over them. As if dancing with a child. Or a doll.

Setting me back down, Victor captures my gaze, his dark eyes widening. "Tell me something, Samantha." His words slither through me like warm honey. Even without knowing the phrase's ending, my body already wants to do anything Victor is about to ask, no matter how much my brain rebels against it.

His smile widens. "Are you—"

"May I cut in?" Cassis injects, his easygoing nonchalance at utter odds with the count's formality. Without waiting for an answer, the younger vampire deftly slips an arm around my waist just as the music starts again. "I wouldn't usually interrupt you, Victor, but I have good money riding on whether Samantha will slap me in the face before the song's end."

"I would not dream of disrupting a wager," Victor says graciously, yielding my hand to Cassis. "Whom do you recommend I bet on?"

"On me, of course." Winking at the count, Cassis starts us back into the dance.

"Was that a smart thing to do?" I ask once I'm able to recapture my breath, the phantom fear of what Victor might have asked of me still turning my stomach. There has to be something that can be done to ward off the vamp's compulsion. "Cut in with Victor, I mean."

"Absolutely not." Cassis steps through me just as Victor had, his thigh brushing the inside of mine. Same move, but different. More teasing than intrusive, and my body knows it. Reminding myself to get back to Victor, I give Cassis a worried glance, but he only smirks. "One advantage of starting out on someone's bad side, however, is that he can't dislike me any more than he already does."

21

Sam

To my relief, Count Victor doesn't so much as look in my direction for the rest of the night, though that could be because he literally has a swarm of vamps and demis following him around like obsessed bees. Not that he could easily get to me with Cassis somehow always there, spinning me into a dance or snatching drinks, or pulling me away from a dull conversation with a hand in the small of my back. At first, I shy away from him, the memory of his teeth in my neck, the pure hatred in his eyes as he overpowered me, too much. But finally, perhaps some animal part of me enjoying the endorphin rush of playing with a predator, I give in to the allure. The fun of the moment. Cassis is simply too handsome to resist forever.

Cassis finally leaves my side only to get behind the piano, the notes singing from beneath his fingers quieting the room even more quickly than Victor's voice. As much as I shy away from attention—and the dark, lingering glances that come with it—the male thrives on it. I can see why he'd run a place like Dusk.

The more I start to enjoy myself, the less Ellis seems to—or perhaps I'm just imagining it. *Less* implies he enjoyed the evening to begin with. From what I see of the male, he spends the night propping up a wall, glaring at anyone who accidentally strays too close. Asher and Reese, who I now realize are the only vampire and fae I see together on a regular basis, remain on quiet intense alert.

Stepping out of the ballroom into the night air, I shiver as the wind ruffles my hair against my neck, the cold sending goose bumps down my bare back. Walking beside me, Cassis takes off his tuxedo jacket and puts it over my shoulders without a word, then sticks his hands into his pockets and gazes up at the stars. Though it carries no body heat, the jacket smells of his delicious spicy cologne, and I have to stop myself from inhaling audibly. The sky is clear and rich, just like the day I first met Ellis. The day everything in my life changed.

"Why did you do all that?" I ask Cassis, who's keeping step with me as I head back to the barracks. Walking me home? Not something I'd have dared allow in my previous world, but now the thought makes me giddy, my sex clenching hungrily at possibilities my mind is afraid to consider.

Cassis's attention stays on the stars, his cool presence brushing my skin without touching it. "Do what?"

"Save me from Victor. Keep me company the whole night. Get me a dress."

A small confused frown flickers over his beautiful face, as if I've asked something universally obvious. "Because pissing off Victor is enjoyable. Because I enjoy your company. What was the third question—oh, the dress. Because going to a ball naked is frowned upon."

"I wasn't going to go naked."

"Going in a little plaid skirt and white shirt is even worse," Cassis informs me. "Your lack of appreciation for clothing is actually offensive." Stopping by the first-year barracks—of course he knows where that is—Cassis opens the door for me. Another strange novelty. But I have a feeling that asking him to stop doing that is akin to asking him to stop breathing.

I mean, if breathing is a regular thing for him. I'm still not clear on just how much air vampires need.

Climbing the steps up to the second floor, I feel my heart speed up, the possibilities for the rest of the night unfolding deliciously inside me. We'll come up to my room, stopping just outside my door. There, Cassis will pause in that infuriatingly lazy manner and smile down at me with that heartbreaking, mischievous grin. Then the vampire will run his long fingers along the side of my face, tucking a strand of hair behind my ear. It will be impertinent. Irresistible. My heart will stop, my stomach clenching as he leans down, his powerful lips pressing over mine. And then he'll step into me, just like he did in the dance, except this time instead of propelling us across the dance floor, he'll push me backward into my room. Not stopping until the backs of my thighs hit the bed…

I swallow at the thought. Damn it, but I don't remember ever wanting a man this much before. The newness of the sensation tingles over my skin.

"This is you," Cassis says, and I realize we're already outside my door, just as the movie inside my mind choreographed. A jolt of need makes my breasts feel heavy, my peaked nipples pressing against my gown. My sex tightens as I tip my face up to the male's. Dark hair, a strong jawline, eyes a mixture of mischief and understanding that pierces deep into me without trying. Making me feel like there's no other place in the world Cassis would rather be right now.

Hell, we aren't even touching, and I already feel his energy shooting straight into my core.

"This is me." I smile up at him.

Cassis braces his hand on the door frame, the hard biceps beneath his jacket flexing in a sharp reminder of just how powerful he really is. That beneath all the designer suits and reckless mischief is a history as dark as mine. Darker perhaps. And yet, here he is, standing tall and playing music and giving a grand fuck-you to the world that tried so hard to break him.

When the male lowers his mouth toward me, it's all I can do to keep from moaning as I breath in his cologne. As his lips…

As his lips touch my cheek with butterfly softness and pull away. "Stay safe, Samantha."

Wait. What?

"You don't have to go." My heart stutters at my own words. Never, ever, have I voluntarily invited a man into my room before. Never longed for the pain that comes with fucking. I hadn't realized how vulnerable the invitation would leave me, my palms tingling, my breath held.

Cassis cocks his head, his gaze brushing me with unbridled sensuality. His hand comes up, the soft brush of his fingertips along my cheek nearly bringing me onto my toes. Then, finally, wrapping his fingers around a lock of my hair, Cassis...tugs it like a bloody fourth grader and pulls away.

"Yes, I do," he says, straightening his cuff links. "Thank you for a lovely evening, Samantha."

The words hit me like freezing rain, washing the stupid fairy tale I'd spun in my mind right back into the dirt where it belongs. An idiot. I am an utter, gullible, stupid idiot who deserves everything coming to her. Cassis is a playboy. Charming and wealthy and so attention basking, it would put any cat to shame.

I swallow as the evening repeats itself back to me in refreshing clarity. Cassis dressed me like a toy, playing Victor and me and everybody else in a perfect marionette theater. Entertaining himself. I'd wager my leather jacket that he picks out the outfits of the dancing girls at Dusk just as he picked out my clothing for tonight. I stopped wondering too early why Cassis came to the ball. Had I been smarter, I'd have figured it out.

He came for the show. His own show.

I'm a fucking idiot.

"Samantha." Cassis drops to that low seductive timbre that I know better than to fall for now. "For what it's worth, I am as surprised as you are not to be sliding between your sheets already."

"That makes three of us." Ellis's cold words sound from somewhere to my right.

I step away from Cassis as the storm that is Ellis strides down the long hallway, his blond hair mussed, bow tie undone and hanging in a ribbon of black silk around his neck. The top of his white shirt is open, showing the flare of his chest muscles, like a wild animal who's torn off a collar it never should have been forced to wear.

"Ellis." Cassis grins from his perch against the wall, which makes the darkness in Ellis's eyes flash with yellow lightning. "I was wondering if you were actually bedding down in the first-years' dorm or just curling up on a mat outside the back door. From a hygiene perspective, I'd personally worry about any fleas you might carry. The little buggers do spread quickly in an enclosed space."

"Is there a reason you're still here, Cassis? Last I checked, there is no Victor here for you to provoke further."

My body tightens. I'd have thought hearing Ellis confirm my suspicions would hardly matter at this point, but it's like pouring salt on a wound. Shaking my head, I pin Cassis with a hard gaze. Call me a masochist, but as far as this has gone, I want to know for sure. "Tell me the truth, Cassis. Were you using me tonight to piss Victor off?"

"Yes, of course I was," Cassis says easily. "I just told you as much earlier. I don't lie—it's one of my faults."

"Right." I swallow the pain gripping my throat and give both the males a conjured smile. My own damn fault. My aching, tearing heart is my own stupid fault. And I'll never let it happen again. "You're right, Cassis, you did." I mean to add a good night to that sentence, but my eyes start to sting, so I disappear into my room instead.

22

Sam

"Get up."

I groan and ignore the noise. I'm exhausted. The very effort of *not* crying in the dark like some stupid little girl stole whatever strength I had left after the Cassis disaster. The feat of falling asleep was a distant second, and I'd be surprised if I've gotten more than three hours thus far. My calves hurt after wearing heels last night, and my entire body feels thick and heavy.

"Get. Up."

Sitting up, I take a swing at whatever is talking.

An iron-hard grip captures my wrist midmotion, jerking me to the floor hard enough that my shoulder screams in protest.

"What the fucking hell?" I yell, my eyes finally focusing on Ellis, who's looming over me, black joggers and tight sleeveless shirt showing off a full range of corded muscles. His white hair is pulled back tightly, the lines of his beautiful face sculpted with anger. "Go disappear into whatever bloody hole you're crawled out of, Ellis. It's liberty today."

"Not for you." The male's golden eyes flash, as if it's me hazing him, not the other way around. "Training time, witch."

"Says who?"

"Says me." Ellis turns toward the door. "Be on the pitch in five minutes."

"Or else what, you'll be really, *really* grumpy?"

"Make me wait and find out," Ellis barks over his shoulder, the door slamming in his wake.

"Trouble with your boyfriend?" Bernadette asks, a small smile on her full lips. She looks as fresh and stunning as always, her red hair braided down her back, green eyes set off by long, mascaraed lashes—though I'm certain she stayed at the ball until it closed in the wee hours of the morning. The vampires rarely sleep at all, and the vamp demis need no more than a couple of hours to feel refreshed.

Which reinforces my suspicions that the Academy made us room together just to make each other's lives miserable.

I give her a sugar-sweet smile that I know she hates. "That's how he expresses his love."

Yes, I know I'm purposely irritating Bernadette. Which may be stupid and childish, but I won't be knocking Ellis on his ass any time soon, and I want to take a swing at someone. Even a verbal one. Fair? No. Do I care after last night? Fuck no.

Bernadette's manicured brow twitches, and the one damn time I need her to snarl right back at me, her large eyes soften in sympathy. "Look, none of us particularly likes you, Sam, but even we think letting Ellis have his fun with you is messed up. I mean, there is a line."

"Oh, I'm pretty sure Ellis takes no pleasure in our training," I say, pulling on my workout gear and trying hard not to hate my roommate for cruising through all the physical training by virtue of her vamp blood while I sweat. We're on different paths anyway. Bernadette wants to attract the attention of someone important— like Victor—who could invite her into a vampire clan, whereas I am many years past the please-your-foster-family-so-they-keep-you bullshit. I don't need anyone. I just want to survive this purgatory so

I can get back to normal human life with the one person I should be relying on—myself. "In fact, I'm fairly certain that watching me trip over my own feet is the bastard's personal version of hell."

Bernadette barks a laugh, and I know we're done with the whole empathy thing. "I can't tell where your ignorance ends and your stupidity begins. I mean, everyone knows Ellis could kill half the Academy if he put his mind to it, and is wearing a cadet's uniform because he pissed someone off. But that's not even the interesting part." She leans forward. "Word on the street is that Ellis is one of the Talon king's bastards. The dark son the king dispatches when someone needs to be brought back in line. Or taken out permanently. If even a part of what I've heard about him is true, making people suffer isn't just a by-product of Ellis's existence, it's his fucking job. And do you imagine for a second that a male like that doesn't enjoy it?"

Yeah. I'm done listening. Poisonous as Bernadette is, I wouldn't put it past her to invent things about Ellis just to make him seem like an even bigger asshole—as if he needs any more help in that department.

Without bothering to reply, I grab a sweatshirt and pull it over my training uniform—unlike the rest of the Academy, I feel the cold just fine, thank you very much—and get myself out to the pitch. The sun is just coming over the pines in thin morning rays, long trails of mist still shifting over the grass.

Ellis is already going through exercises as I come up to sand-covered ground, his body moving smoothly against the background of the rising sun like some scene from a martial arts movie. Except that unlike the movies, Ellis's forms are for real, each punch and kick and block vibrating with a constrained power that should be impossible when fighting air.

For a moment, I just stand at the edge of the sand and watch him fight his phantoms, his low ponytail snapping in the wind with each movement. He looks almost content. And then he turns toward me, and all those glorious movements disappear right along with that content expression, as if my appearance has brought him crashing back down to an unwelcome reality.

Picking up two glorified sticks lying on the sideline, Ellis tosses one to me hard enough that the wood raps my fingers when I catch it.

"Are we playing at Teenage Mutant Ninja Turtles?" Just longer than my arm, the polished wood is shaped like a dull sword but is heavier than it should be. Frowning at the handle, I discover that the toy sword's core has been weighted with metal.

"You are learning how to use a sword," he says. While he's never exactly nice, his voice is rougher than usual today, the storm in his golden eyes barely contained. Weighing me with his gaze, he shakes his head as if finding me wanting. "Copy my footwork."

"Seriously?" I blink at the length of wood in my hand. "Are you insane? Because no one uses swords anymore. If this is a new type of torment—" I cut off as the tip of Ellis's practice sword suddenly presses into the fragile cartilage of my windpipe, the hard set of his jaw warning that he is one hair's breadth away from leaning into the blade.

Yes, apparently, seriously.

"Vampires must lose their head or all their blood to die, but a well-placed cut will slow them down long enough for you to get away. A wooden stake is effective only if you strike the heart directly. Either way, it starts with good footwork. Is there a reason you're looking at me like I'm speaking in another language?"

"If this is actually about self-defense, how about a gun?"

"Have we not had this discussion already?" Ellis snaps, his Scottish accent growing thicker. "Besides being impossible to bring into Talon or discharge safely in populated areas, guns are simply ineffective against vampires. A vampire's heart beats once every few minutes at best, so the bit of damage from an average bullet is an annoyance more than anything. Beheadings, on the other hand, work well. Get your sword up."

"Is this about Cassis—" I yelp as Ellis's blade raps my upper arm hard enough to send a zing of numbing pain down to my fingers.

"This is about the fact that my damn punishment is to keep your arse alive, and you aren't making that easy. So I've no intention of making it easy on you either." Stepping in close, Ellis hooks my sword with his and glares down from his towering height. "Now, you are going to follow each and every one of my steps, or we are going to run for an hour and then start from the beginning. Is there any part of that you had trouble understanding?"

I bite down my first instinct, which is to tell Ellis exactly where he can shove my understanding. "No, you're clear as glass. Crystal clear, in fact," I say, giving the male a mock salute. If Ellis expects me to cower before his mighty anger, he has another thing coming.

His jaw tightens, but he waits for me to take up a position beside him before starting us into motion. Into lunges, to be exact. Forward lunges. Reverse lunges. Lunges with the practice sword held high. Lunges with that bloody sword in whatever position makes my arms tremble, my thighs burning with enough hellfire to roast marshmallows.

"High parry," Ellis calls relentlessly, each word like an extra weight hung around my neck. Despite the cold morning, sweat drips down my scalp, snaking down the groove of my spine. My boots slip on the sand. "Low. Lunge. Up. High."

I do as he says. I lunge and I parry and—despite my cracks about ninja turtles—I put everything into my trembling muscles. A peace offering of sorts.

Except Ellis is not feeling like peace, it seems, his voice as unrelenting as his cold face. As if he isn't rooting for me to succeed but waiting for me to fail.

Stop letting Bernadette under your skin, I remind myself as I double over for breath, my hands braced against my thighs. I hurt. Hurt so bad I would voluntarily go running now just to get a break from the blade work.

"Reset," Ellis orders, his demand lashing at me just as the tip of my sword touches the sand. I have to fight with all my strength not to follow the damn thing down.

"Need. A. Break." My words come in desperate gasps, my lungs burning as I gulp air.

Ellis's golden gaze captures mine, and my heart stops at the ice I see there. At the wooden blade he sends sailing at my skull with enough force to crack open the bone.

"You think anyone cares?" His eyes flash as a rush of fear-driven adrenaline forces my arm up to parry the blow. The clack of wood on wood is so hard, I feel it echoing through my bones. "You think vampires get tired? You think they negotiate for a more convenient rendezvous? Reset."

Ellis doesn't wait to see whether I'm ready—which I'm not— and when his sword raps against my ribs, a shout of pain escapes me.

"Are you insane?" I demand.

"No, you are," he barks. Unlike me, the male isn't so much as breathing hard, his lithe, powerful body seeming to be everywhere without exertion. "If you can't be bothered to curb your recklessness, tell me why the hell I should be doing it for you. Reset."

I'm smart enough to mind the order and block his blade before it strikes me again in the same spot. Again. And again. My heart pounds, the morning sun now shining into my eyes, my body somehow blazing hot while the fingers wrapped around my sword are numb and chilled. The walls of forest on every side of us watch in cool, impartial silence. The realization that there is—there will be —no end to Ellis's assault spreads through my blood like acid. No end, no point, no anything but the *clack clack clack* of useless wooden sticks while my muscles tremble and my breaths come in knifelike puffs of cold air.

Nothing on the streets could ever have prepared me for this— not fighting off bullies or escaping foster brothers. Not even the slaps and much worse doled out by drunk men in the name of discipline. Nothing could ever have prepared me for Ellis.

"Reset," he snaps after landing another blow, this one powering through my parry to slap my shoulder.

"No!" Gripping the wooden sword in both hands, I hurl the damn toy into Ellis's face, the male looking surprised as he catches it on instinct. I gulp a mouthful of air. "I'm done with your games," I shout, not caring that heads are now turning toward us as others in the training yard smell the budding riffs of a juicy conflict. "You want to have a pissing match with Cassis, have at it. Leave me the fuck out of it."

"Cassis is irrelevant." Ellis throws the blade at my feet, his nostrils flaring. "Pick it up." His voice drops. "Pick it up, or I will enjoy what happens next a great deal more than you will."

I raise my chin, using what little strength I have to straighten my back before the storm that is Ellis, to enunciate each one of my words. "Go. To. Hell."

Silence settles over the training yard, as if everyone sucks in a collective breath. For a moment, Ellis just stands there, frozen. But then he moves.

No, he pounces.

One moment, we are both on our feet, and the next, he is on top of me, one foot sweeping out my ankle to throw me flat on my face in the sand.

23

Sam

S and scrapes against my face, rushing into my nose as I inhale—which I can only do once before Ellis's knee presses right into floating ribs, bending me back like a bow. I bite back a scream, the world darkening around the edges as my heart races. Pounds. Each squeeze of my heart dumping another doze of terror through me.

I'm on the sand, except I'm not. I'm somewhere in a corner of a room, cowering as a man with work boots and stains of beer and vomit on his pants kicks me in the ribs. Blood pours into my mouth as I bite my lip, my small body flailing uselessly.

Something shifts and now instead of my ribs, a heavy weight pins me utterly to the ground, a man's forearm coming around my throat.

"This is how quickly a vampire is going to take you down, Devinee," Ellis hisses into my ear, bringing my reality right back into focus. "He is going to take you down and rip into your jugular, and then he's going to drink all the blood pouring through that little, fragile body of yours. Now, tap out and get the hell off my pitch like you wanted."

No. Tucking my chin to protect my neck, I tighten every muscle in my body. Ellis might have beaten me, but I'm not…not throwing myself at his mercy. As fine a point as that seems, refusing to give a bully the satisfaction of knowing that he crushed my mind along with my body is the only thing I have left today. And Ellis can't have that.

"Tap out, cadet, you've lost this one." Asher's quiet demand barely registers though the haze. "You should be well beyond childish tantrums."

Ellis's body presses harder into mine, taking away any space my lungs have to expand for breath. Just as I think my world will finally slip into wonderful darkness, he grips my wrist, forcing my arm into motion. *Tap. Tap. Tap.*

Bits of sand fly into the air along with the remains of my dignity as Ellis puppeteers me through surrender.

Then he lifts off me, and I *run.*

I BARGE INTO MY ROOM, the tears I refuse to shed anywhere on this Academy ground stinging my eyes. Bernadette is still there, her I-told-you-so look raking my soul like nails on a chalkboard.

"You were right," I say, grabbing my bag and stuffing a blanket inside it. "The asshole enjoys it."

I don't even know which "it" I hate Ellis more for now, the *training* or the surrender. Grabbing a bottle of water, I cringe as it burns its way down my sore throat. The avalanche of emotions nearly knocks me off my feet as the harsh reality slaps my face.

It isn't Ellis who's at fault for any of this. It's me. Because some small part of me had started to trust the male, just as another part had played make-believe with what Cassis thought of me. I was the one who broke my own rules. And now, now I've gotten what I deserve.

"You know you can't actually leave Talonswood, don't you?" Bernadette says, cocking her head as she jerks her chin toward my bag. "The woods aren't safe, not beyond the running trails. And then there's the whole island thing. This is a prison, witch, in case you haven't worked that out already."

"Yeah. I worked it out." Shouldering my bag, I grab a heel of bread and my water bottle. I know better than to try to escape just now, with no plan, no supplies. But I also know that I need to be alone. To lick my wounds. To remind myself that no one *made me* trust them. I walked into the fucking trap all by myself. And I will never do it again.

"Sam," Bernadette calls to my retreating back, and I don't know what makes me stop at the edge of the door instead of going forward. "I'll cover for you until this evening, but that's it. Don't think I'm risking my ass for a witch."

I shrug indifferently and head out. Whether the demi keeps her word about covering or not, that's her choice. From now on, I'm relying on me and me alone.

Pulling my leather jacket tighter around myself, I slip out the back door of the barracks and into the woods. After the were and hunter encounter a few weeks ago, I had no intention of venturing past the exercise trails even without Bernadette's reminder, but given how much everyone around here seems to love running, there are miles and miles of these to choose from.

Despite the early hour, the forest is full of shadows, light struggling to slip through the dense green crown of pines, oaks, and maples. Gripping the straps of my pack, I search for one dark and large enough to let me curl up just for a bit by myself, something deep and cave-like and private. Nothing feels right, not for the first mile of the hike. Nor the second. After what has to be an hour of trudging around the circular trails, I finally find a place at the base of a large oak, several of its long branches dropping low to form a little cocoon.

Climbing inside, I inhale the sweet forest air, cringing at how much the scent reminds me of Ellis. As if he followed me in phantom form. Pulling out my blanket, I wrap the wool around myself as I curl into a ball, the rush of pain and frustration finally slamming into me as the cold seeps farther into my abused body.

Though in truth, I have no one but myself to blame. I was an idiot to think anyone here would be different than everyone else I know. Cassis used me as a pawn to annoy Count Victor and piss off Ellis. And Ellis—he's exactly who Bernadette said he was: a male who enjoys inflicting torment. A bully of the supernatural kind, who has the skill and will and opportunity to beat me down before the whole school.

Taking a shaking breath, I rub my hands over my cheeks, relieved to find the skin dry. I've trained myself to keep the tears in, and that, at least, I haven't surrendered yet. A small victory, but worth holding on to.

About thirty minutes after nuzzling down into my makeshift cave, a sudden crack behind jerks me back to reality. I'm no longer alone, I realize with growing dread. Damn bloody runners. The downside of having stayed to the safe parts of the woods is that other beings have the same idea.

I hold myself still, hoping that whoever is using the trail will pass without noticing my little pity party. And if not, well, what's a bit more hazing from a demi?—I'll take that over a were or hunter any day.

I catch sight of red braided hair for a moment before it disappears, the wilderness going quiet again. Quieter. For all my awareness of living in the city, the smells and sights of the wilderness are still new. Unnerving.

Especially when the whole place seems to suddenly go silent and still.

A second later, I barely have a chance to gasp as someone tackles me from behind. No one near as big as Ellis, but still lean and strong. When a familiar scent of lilac shampoo fills my nose, the red braid I saw earlier snaps into place, a mix of recognition, relief, and annoyance creating their own cocktail.

Bernadette.

"Fuck off," I shout, struggling to shake her from my back while she recreates the match Ellis inflicted on me earlier. Pressing me face-first into the ground, the demi grapevines her legs over mine until I'm stretched flat and flopping like a fish. Fury races through my blood, heating it to a boil. Gathering all my remaining strength, I buck as hard as I can. "Get the fuck off!"

Bernadette laughs, riding me like a bronco, her arm snaking around the sensitive curve of my throat. When her mouth comes close to the pulsing vein in my neck, however, the fury shifts to fear with blinding speed. I freeze.

"Oh, don't worry, witch," the girl purrs into my ear. "I won't be tasting your blood today. Count Victor wouldn't want seconds."

The weight atop me shifts slightly, then I hear more than feel something hard smashing the side of my head. Pain explodes though my skull, the world blinking in and out of darkness, my body going limp.

"Shit." Bernadette rolls off me and grabs my hair, pulling my face out of the dirt. "You still alive?"

Balling my hand into a fist, I swing at her face, as surprised as she looks when my knuckles connect with something.

"Bitch." Whipping around me, Bernadette snakes her arm around my neck from behind, and uses the choke hold to force me to my feet. "You are a never-ending source of trouble, but perhaps it's time that you turn into something useful for a change, don't you think?"

Ignoring my attempt to claw at her arm, Bernadette marches me forward, half forcing me into motion, half keeping me upright. I try to clear my head to think straight, but my body is shot, my head one big pounding ball of confusion. Bernadette. Following me. Attacking me. Leading me where?

That last is answered sooner than I'd like as we turn off the trail and into the dense woods, branches slapping my face and arms, roots rising up to trip me. Bernadette's hand just tightens even further when I stumble, gripping hard enough to bruise. My heart pounds with each step. The mantra of every self-defense video plays inside my head, reminding me to never let an attacker take you to a secondary location. Especially when that secondary location reveals itself to be a full-on cage bolted down into a stone. Right in the middle of the damn forest.

"It's for weres," Bernadette says, pleased. She takes off the open lock and shoves me inside the cage hard enough that I hit the bars and fall. "You know, the little fae-blooded ass wipes who can't control their shifting."

A soft moan escapes me as I fight to stay conscious. From the corner of my eye, I see Bernadette pull a rope from her pack and make short work of tying my hands behind my back. Before I can ask if there's a point of tying me up inside a cage, she stuffs a rag into my mouth and closes the padlock with a final loud *click*.

"They don't give students a key, in case you were wondering," she says, walking away.

24

Ellis

*E*llis buried his fist in the canvas punching bag, Sam's shout of pain echoing through him. He shoved it away. This was why he was sent here, wasn't it? Another dirty assignment, just like the others he'd done for his father in the past four centuries. He was here to break the witch to bridle and rebuild her into something useful to Talon—something loyal to Talon.

At the very least, to rebuild her into something that wouldn't get dead within the first five minutes of meeting reality. A witch, rare as they were now, was too precious a commodity to waste on a chance encounter with a thirsty vamp.

Thump thump thump.

The sound of his fist striking its target echoed through the gym, focusing Ellis's ragged thoughts. Downing out his agitation over questioning himself. He'd been right this morning. He'd been fully and totally right.

Ellis wasn't here to be Sam's friend. Wasn't here to savor the way her hazel eyes sparkled with life and rebellion despite everything life had thrown at her. To be tortured by thoughts of her sinfully sweet curves under that red dress, her fiery hair brushing her neck as she danced and laughed. To remember what it felt like the one time she'd allowed him to lift her into his arms, to cradle her small, warm body against his chest as he carried her through the woods, her sweet citrusy scent filling his lungs.

For the first time since he could remember, Ellis had slept without nightmares that night.

But that wasn't what he was here for. He was here to keep the witch alive long enough for the ruby egg his father held to hatch.

If the witch didn't understand that stubborn rebellion alone would not protect her—and seeing how she'd spent last night pissing off Victor before nearly inviting a vampire into her bedchamber, she did not, in fact, understand— that was Ellis's own fault. And this morning, he'd taken the first step to correcting the oversight.

Ellis punched the bag again, as he'd been doing for hours. He wasn't Devinee's friend. He was her jailer. Her tormentor. The one called in to bring her to heel. Because that was what Ellis did. What he was good at. What he was good for.

Thump thump thump.

Spinning around, Ellis sank the heel of his bare foot into the punching bag, knocking the thing straight off the hinges. Flying through the training hall, the bag crashed into the opposite wall, bits of drywall and plaster spraying from the newly created hole.

"Want to tell me what this is all about?" Asher asked, and Ellis spun around, cursing himself for not realizing that his brother had entered the room some time back. Inexcusable. It was the witch. He'd never have allowed such a mistake before he'd met Samantha Devinee.

Moving over to the second punching bag in the row of three, Ellis punched the new target with enough force that his skinned knuckles left splotches of blood on the canvas. "Your bag can't hang right," he said over his shoulder. "I think that's rather plain."

Ellis pulled back his fist, stopping when Asher grabbed the bag and held it out of comfortable striking range, his tawny eyes all too knowing.

"You want to try that again?" he said quietly, the attitude of an

Academy instructor coming through loud and clear. Ellis's brother was altogether civilized nowadays. Rules and forms, grading journals, and official balls. Asher had been the strategist once, his passion for victory and a new world of peace between species burning as bright as the sun. That was before Sienna had murdered Asher's lover before his eyes, claiming that it was a witch—not a fae—Asher was destined to be with.

"Your equipment is a piece of shite, sir," Ellis said, jerking the punching bag free of Asher's grasp. "If you'd prefer to show me how things are done, I'd be happy to step into the cage with you right now." He jerked his chin toward the fighting cage in the corner of the gym, its octagonal shape a tribute to the human form of entertainment.

"I'm not going to get into the ring with you, Ellis," Asher said, that cool tone especially infuriating against the backdrop of fury rolling through Ellis's veins.

"Afraid you'd lose?" Ellis snarled.

"I'm not afraid I'd lose," Asher said with that horrid calm. "I'm certain of it. Which is why I'm not going to start a fight I can't win. Want to tell me why the hell you did?"

Devinee.

"What gives you the impression that I lost?" Ellis asked, and this time when he went to strike the bag, Asher let him.

"Fair point." Asher rocked back on his heels. "You are exactly the kind of male who'd go out of his way to ensure that the woman he was falling in love with hates his guts."

Ellis's fist froze in midair, Asher's words hitting him upside the head and scrambling his brain for a moment. Ellis tolerated the witch on a good day and barely stopped himself from wringing her neck on a usual one. "I don't know who you were watching this morning, but it wasn't me." He punched the bag again as if to punctuate his point.

"The witch has no sense of self-preservation," Asher said, fortunately dropping the ridiculous assertion. "That's a problem for me. Fighting through fear and hardship is courage. Fighting just for fighting's sake or because you can't read the battlefield—"

"You think I don't know that?" Ellis huffed. "It's a good thing Father sent me here, because I don't know how I've managed to wipe my own ass all these centuries without your guidance."

Ellis saw Asher snatch for his neck before the male's hand connected with his throat, but he allowed it to happen. Allowed Asher to pin him against the wall like a pup.

"And now you are baiting me, Ellis," Asher's eyes flashed. "You want to punish yourself? Fine. But keep your mouth in check and stop trying to manipulate me into doing it for you."

Ellis bared his teeth. Asher was wrong. Ellis wasn't looking for punishment; he was looking to be left the hell alone.

"What are you going to do next?" Asher asked, releasing Ellis as if the incident never happened. Unlike Ellis, Asher knew exactly when to push, when to back off—which had made him a great general in the mortal military until he got tired of faking his death on a regular basis to avoid human suspicion and taken the Academy position. And, damn it, Ellis was jealous. Jealous of Asher's control. Of Reese's ability to shut off emotion. Of Cassis's brazen hedonism.

"I hate to interrupt what is clearly an intimate moment." Reese's clipped British tones cut between Ellis and Asher. "But has anyone seen Ms. Devinee this morning?"

Asher and Ellis spun at once, Ellis's breath coming in winded puffs. "She went to the barracks after throwing a tantrum on the pitch. Keeping track of snot-nosed cadets is supposed to be your job, Reese."

"I was under the impression that keeping this particular cadet in line was directly your responsibility. Yet here you are, arguing with a punching bag. Though in truth, I can't say I altogether blame you for seeking out something a little closer to your own intellect to play with."

"Is the witch not in her room?" Asher bladed his body to get between Ellis and Reese. Not a bad idea given that a fight between two assassins would not end well. "Sam's roommate requested permission to stay in with her while the girl recovered from training. I granted it."

"That was my understanding as well," said Reese, the warrior's muscles tense as if he too gave a damn about the witch's safety. Ellis wasn't sure whether he wanted to thank or throttle the male for that. "The demi was keeping an eye on the witch while Ellis entertained himself with leaving holes in walls. But when I checked just now, I found both the girls missing. Quinn too."

Ellis's world stopped. "All three are gone?" he demanded, shifting into wolf form before even hearing an answer.

2 5

Sam

I only realize I'd passed out when I open my eyes to discover the sun has moved. Along with a splitting headache, I'm acutely aware of two familiar voices coming closer to me. Male and female, neither making an effort to keep themselves from being noticed. Out here, there is no one to notice anything.

"A tribute," says the female. Bernadette. Shit. "For Count Victor. Something that seemed to catch his eye."

"And why exactly is a demi packaging up a present for the count?" Quinn asks with a thick condescension that makes it clear he both knows the answer and enjoys rubbing Bernadette's face in it. I mean, even I know the answer—Bernadette wants to catch the count's attention. Apparently, however, she couldn't get past Quinn.

I hope that's a point in my favor.

"I thought he would find a witch's blood a pleasant diversion from his everyday. A delicacy." Bernadette clears her throat as if she's in a bloody job interview, except that the demi wears her emotions on her sleeve. Desperation. Hope. Just a dash of fear. "It's a demonstration of the kind of initiative, attention, and loyalty he can expect from me should he consider adopting me into his clan."

The tree branches shift, the pair now coming into view. My heart starts to hammer. Quinn wears his blue uniform jacket, his black hair combed back neatly from his forehead. For a brief moment, I consider calling out to him for help—but I'm not a dumbass. If the male is going to help me—doubtful, given how openly Bernadette speaks to him, but theoretically possible—he'll do it because kidnapping is undesirable, not because I asked him nicely. Hell, he'd probably enjoy watching me plead if given half a chance.

Keeping my eyes open just a small crack, I feign ongoing unconsciousness, the effort of keeping my breathing steady over the gag making me dizzy.

Quinn's cool dark eyes brush along me before he turns to Bernadette and glares down at her. "Let me get this straight, Yalls. You want me to believe you single-handedly kidnapped Devinee from the Academy with no one the wiser?"

"No." Bernadette flashes a smile. "The witch ran. Got her feelings hurt by Ellis and dashed off to cry herself to sleep in the woods. I simply capitalized on the opportunity."

"And when she fails to return, the disappearance can be blamed on weres." Quinn tips his head, considering. "And how many others know of this?"

"That she ran off? *Everyone.*" I hear more than see the grin filling Bernadette's words. "And now that she's secure, we can move her anywhere the count would find convenient. No one need ever find the body."

"Of course they'll find her, you idiot half-breed." Quinn rolls his eyes. "The fae wolves will smell her trail as if you lined it with treats. They might smell yours as well."

Bernadette swallows, the confidence of her posture breaking as she wrings her hands. "Then perhaps you might offer your wisdom, Commander. Would…would you like a taste, perhaps?"

Quinn licks his lips, suggesting that Bernadette has found the right angle of attack. Then his mouth closes with a hard snap. "If you are to present something to the count, you don't give him leftovers."

Bernadette is now nodding enthusiastically. "Yes, you're right. Of course. Which is why I didn't try her. Didn't so much as take a sip."

"Excellent." The finality in Quinn's voice makes my breath hitch. Stepping behind Bernadette, the vampire puts his hand on the demi's shoulder, the pair of them now looking down at me. "You did good work today, Bernadette Yalls. Count Victor will be highly pleased with his little treat. It is unfortunate you won't be able to enjoy his gratitude personally."

The flicker of confusion that passes over Bernadette's face lives only a moment—which is as long as the girl herself does. With a sharp snap of his hand, Quinn turns her head at a fierce angle, her thick red braid making one last flick as the sound of her snapping neck fills the forest.

"You can stop pretending to be asleep, Samantha." Tossing Bernadette's limp body into the woods, Quinn comes to crouch beside my cage, the tip of his tongue running over his teeth longingly as he stares at the blood trickling down my forehead.

Pulling his attention away with a growl, he slings off his pack, pulling pieces of a firearm out of it.

I scream into my gag.

"Easy, witch." Quinn grins at me, assembling the pieces into a rifle and scope. A strange-looking thing on the barrel completes the monstrosity. "This isn't for you."

I glare at him and struggle against my bindings, knowing that my defiance won't do anything beyond making some of my dried scratches bleed fresh.

"That blood is just going to waste," Quinn says regretfully, as if the two of us are sharing some kind of camaraderie in the matter. "But alas, the count would know. Especially when it's his own son taking a mouthful." He smiles, cocking his head. "You look surprised. Did you not know Victor himself sired me? Did you think my blood ran as bastardly as the idiots who call themselves the cadre? So much to learn. First, though, let's see if we can't bait a bigger fish for our stew, shall we? Ellis does so enjoy your company."

Rising to his feet, Quinn slings his rifle over his shoulder and walks away toward the cliffs, climbing to higher ground and disappearing from view.

The next minutes take hours. Or days. The initial panic over what I just saw is enough to keep my heart racing until I realize that this requires more air than I can pull in through the gag. That my breath must slow if I want to live. With the slowing breaths, however, come flashes of frightening understanding.

Quinn is out there with a sniper rifle, and I am bait. Gagged, but not knocked out. Able to make noise, but not use words. Quinn thinks Ellis will come after me, and he wants me able to draw attention but no more, so that…so that Quinn can kill him.

I struggle against my binds, getting the gag out of my mouth suddenly of the utmost importance. Except my body is too spent to cooperate, each inch of progress taking an eternity. Taking too long. Evening begins to lower through the trees, dappled golden light giving way to purple dusk. When a wolf's howl breaks the rustling night sounds, I know I've lost. Though I go still as a rabbit, the wolf comes anyway.

Prowling out of the brush, his golden eyes shining in the setting sun as his snow-white fur stands on end. Each of the predator's steps is filled with power, and, as he spots my cage, he stops. His gnashing teeth would have me frantic for my life if I weren't so frantic for his.

Go away. I glare at the wolf, yelling the words inside my mind. *GO AWAY.*

The wolf shimmers, the air around him swimming like heat above a boiling kettle. Muscles change and elongate until it is Ellis standing before me, still wearing the same training clothes he had on when he destroyed me on the pitch. I'm surprised to see sweat gleaming on his forehead, his chest heaving and eyes shifting wildly as he takes in me, the cage, my gag, his long fingers white-knuckled around his sword handle.

I shake my head, flinging myself against my binds as I try to motion toward the cliffs and shout into the gag. "It's a trap!"

Ellis frowns, taking a step toward me before stopping to crouch into a fighting stance, turning in a slow circle.

Hope spikes my blood for the first time since Bernadette captured me. Which only makes the drop to reality that much harder a heartbeat later.

I don't see or hear the shot until Ellis drops to the ground, a metal dart piercing the side of his neck.

I scream into the gag, quieting only when I see the male's chest still moving. Unconscious, but alive.

Hiking down from the cliffs ten minutes later, Quinn gives me a mock bow as he opens the padlock on my cage and drags Ellis inside. Grabbing a strange set of chainless shackles from his bag, Quinn starts clipping the thick metal rings around Ellis's wrists and ankles. The lack of any actual restraint sends a wave of utter confusion through me, right until I see Ellis—still unconscious—arch in agony as the metal touches his skin.

"Iron," Quinn says levelly, as if he's instructing class. "The full fae do very poorly with iron. It drains them of their life magic. Another thing you should know by now if you were paying attention in class."

I swear at him, the string of curses coming out as nonsense through the gag.

"The tranquilizer will wear off," Quinn continues, clearly enjoying my panic. "There is nothing to be done for that. At the end of the day, there's simply nothing more effective than iron. Iron and time. Like a good stew, draining takes time. But the payoff? A witch and a Talon royal. Delicious." Finishing snapping everything into place, he excuses himself from the cage and reengages the padlock. Then he bids us a good evening and disappears into the night.

26

Sam

I try to get to Ellis across the eight-foot cage floor, finally managing to poke him in the shoulder with my foot. The male flinches but doesn't wake.

Come on, Ellis. I poke him again and again and again, until finally, the male's eyes open. Then widen in realization.

His muscles all bunch together, launching him toward me with Herculean effort. Yanking the gag out of my mouth, he collapses to his hands and knees, pain-filled breaths escaping him as he pulls the dart out of the side of his neck. "Hold on, Devinee."

I gulp air hungrily as Ellis reaches for my binds, though the movement is plainly painful for him.

"Bernadette," I start, the words spilling from me before he even asks. The trick. The plan. The murder. The bait. Ellis takes it all in, the lack of emotion on his face as terrifying as the words I'm saying. "Why aren't you—"

"Surprised?" Ellis asks. "Because I've lived enough centuries to hear worse." He brushes strong hands along my numb body, the contact sending little bits of reassurance through me. "I have the knot undone. It will hurt when I release it and all the blood rushes back."

"Since when do you notice when I hurt? Arg!" I bite back a yelp in spite of Ellis's warning, the numbed nerves screaming themselves awake.

"I notice every single time." His answer to my rhetorical question is so quiet, I'm not sure it's even meant for me. And right now, I don't care, not with liquid fire pouring through my limbs.

Getting a hand behind my back, Ellis eases me into a sitting position against the side of the cage, his hand lingering on my shoulder as if afraid I might topple otherwise.

"What happens now?" I ask.

Taking hold of my chin, he examines the gash Bernadette's rock left on my forehead, his probing fingers pressing into my scalp. "Now Quinn spins a tale for Asher about me having found you so no one comes looking. By morning, the iron will have drained me enough that I'll barely be able to sit unassisted—and that's when the bloody bastard will come back. It's all a game to please Count Victor. Quinn thinks he can gain favor by delivering a witch and a fae on a proverbial platter." Ellis brushes his thumb over my forehead a final time, the concern in his face too genuine for comfort, too tempting for my aching body. "This could use some stitches, but I don't think the bone is broken. Let's see how the rest of your body is holding up."

I snort softly. The rest of me is one big bruise—in large part courtesy of the male now crouching beside me. Not that I want to bring up the morning *training* just now. Pushing his hands away, I cross my arms over my chest.

For a moment, Ellis looks like he's about to argue, but then he gives me a nod of acknowledgment and settles himself against the cage bars opposite me. With one knee bent and his forearms braced over his muscled thigh, he looks like he's lounging in a common room somewhere without a care in the world. I'd believe the act if not for the pain behind those golden eyes, the slight tightening of his mouth every time he shifts his shackled wrists.

For a few minutes, we sit without saying a word, and I wrap my jacket tightly around myself to ward off the growing chill. Why am I the only one to ever be cold around here? "Why did you come after me?" I ask finally. "If you're so smart and know the dangers, why even bother tracking down a witch?"

Ellis gives me a grin that doesn't touch his pale eyes. "You know why, Devinee. Keeping you alive is my punishment. I would get a worse fate yet if I let something happen to you."

"Worse fate than this?" I gesture around the cage.

"Of course. The worst thing that could happen to me here is death." He turns away, surveying the cage while the look in his eyes says his mind is somewhere else entirely. For some reason, it's all I can do to keep from reaching out to him, trying to uncover what it is that he fears. He tracks a large silhouetted owl winging across the twilight sky. "These cages get inspected regularly, so Quinn will need to move us in the morning. When he comes, I need you to play possum. Broken, docile, too spent to fight. Right up until he gets the cage open. Then you run like hell. Get back to the Academy or—even better—to Cassis. Don't stop. I will keep them distracted. Can you find your way?"

"You don't think Quinn will chase me?" I say, even though that isn't the question I really want to ask.

"Oh, he'll want to. But I will put up enough trouble to buy you time. The last thing Quinn will want to risk is letting me stay alive—and I can be very persistent in that regard."

"Yeah. No. Come up with a better plan. Gallant as it sounds, you aren't going to lay down your life to buy me a chance to run."

"I'm not?" Ellis's voice is as dry as mine.

"No. And we both know it, so cut the crap."

The male swallows, his eyes on the forest again. "Yes," he agrees too easily. "You are right, of course. I'm certain I can best Quinn. He's young and powerful, though untrained. But run anyway. I don't need an audience when I fight."

I stare at him, knowing he's lying. Telling me whatever I want to hear just so… just so…I run? Save myself?

"Can you stop with the games?" My control over my emotions snaps like a bow string, the rage and fear all spilling into my blood at once. My breaths quicken, becoming ragged. "Tell the bloody truth, Ellis! Why did you come after me? What am I that someone wants me so badly, you won't back off?"

"I don't owe you anything, Devinee," Ellis says, his voice changing. Hardening. "Much less the truth."

Closing his eyes, he leans his head back against the bars, his beautiful face so strained that I fight the ridiculous urge to crouch beside him and run a cool hand over his forehead where beads of sweat form despite the chill. On his forearms, angry red streaks are starting to creep out from beneath the iron shackles. With his eyes closed and his muscles tight, he looks almost vulnerable. Like a sleeping wolf.

"I didn't tap, Ellis." The words spill out of me, though I had no plans to rehash this morning. The words burn as I say them. "But you made it look to everyone like I surrendered."

"Yes, I'm aware." Ellis's eyes stay closed, his words a sleepy Scottish drawl. "You were going to get injured, not just hurt, if I let you indulge in your stubbornness much longer."

"You could just have stopped."

"No, I couldn't have." Ellis shifts his weight to get more comfortable. "It would have set a bad precedent for us both. And, given that the point of the lesson was to teach you your limits, not very productive. I cut our losses."

I wait for him to say more, but he doesn't, the owls in the distance hooting companionably in the silence.

"Was it so very hard?" he asks finally, his eyes now open but too deep in thought to read. "To admit that you were at your limit? Did you think you'd be telling me something I didn't know?"

I open my mouth to snap something at him, but night has drained the squabble from me. "When you're small and weak like me, sometimes not begging is the only thing you have left."

There's a resigned sigh, and Ellis stops talking again, opening his mouth only once when I shiver, but shutting it without saying a word. The silence hangs heavy between us, and I can tell that though the male is done speaking, he isn't done thinking. Not at all.

"Does any of this—the training, you being a general asshole, whatever it is you and Cassis have going on—have to do with the mark on my palm?" I ask finally. Maybe this time, I'll actually get answers. "Or the ginormous ruby you wanted me to steal?"

Ellis's eyes shift to me, moonlight glancing off his hard jaw and high cheekbones, golden eyes gleaming. For a moment, he looks more like the animal than the man. "I'll tell you—for a price. You let me touch you."

My spine stiffens, every benefit of the doubt I've extended to him now spiraling down the drain. Of course. Men, males—especially those who are used to power—are all alike. "Let's call it what it is. You want to fuck me."

"Let's call it what it is," Ellis agrees evenly. "I said I wanted to touch you. You added the rest. Say yes or don't. My price stands."

"No."

He nods and closes his eyes again, his breath evening as if napping. Accepting no for an answer? Or just bidding his time?

I bite my lip. I'm not a virgin. Though I've never had sex for pleasure, it isn't as though men haven't taken me before, and the truth is that if Ellis decides to force it, there won't be a thing I could do to stop him. At least this way, I'll have something in return. I grit my teeth. What's a bit more pain and humiliation by now? "Fine," I say quickly before my courage fails. "You can…you can do what it is you want to do."

"Prove it." Ellis's eyes stay closed. "Take off your jacket."

Uh-huh. I do it, putting the jacket carefully on the floor of the cage and shivering in the cold. Ellis's nostrils flare slightly as he inhales, the corners of his lips tugging up.

"Why—"

"I can smell you," he informs me without moving a muscle. "Now the shirt too, please."

"Don't you want to open your eyes and watch the show?"

Ellis opens his eyes, his golden gaze gripping mine and staying there while I peel the shirt off my body, my skin heating. My nipples poke through the thin white bra that I should have thrown out years ago, but he doesn't break my gaze to look at them. Which somehow makes my blood simmer even hotter. Why a chiseled immortal like Ellis, who could have his pick of women, is bothering with a short nobody like me, I have no idea—then again, it isn't as if there are many females in the cage to choose from.

"All right, now, talk," I say.

"I said I wanted to touch you, not just look." Straightening his legs across the floor of the cage, Ellis pats his lap.

2 7

Sam

I make myself crawl toward Ellis, hating how much my body wants to know the feel of him even as my mind knows that I'm nothing but a sex toy to amuse a wolf. And yet my traitorous sex clenches as I inhale the male's clean wild scent, beads of moisture soaking into my panties.

Ellis smiles, the rare sight making my stomach flutter, and I suddenly suspect he can smell my arousal.

My face heats. Well, if he can, he'll also know that it comes with a healthy dose of hatred.

I'm stiff as a board as I settle onto his lap. The feel of his hard thighs beneath my backside makes me aware of every awkward curve of my body beside the powerful perfection of his. I've been on a man's lap before, mostly in foster care—and soon learned that it is the last place I ever want to be again.

Ellis's arms come around me, pulling me into his warm chest.

Right. Here we go. My heart pounds as I make my mind go blank, casting my thoughts into numbness. Imagining that I'm watching a scene happening to someone else. Someone who isn't wrong to enjoy the feel of the muscled thighs beneath her, who is free to savor the little jolts of heat wherever skin meets skin.

Shifting me until my head fits perfectly into the grove of his shoulder, Ellis brushes his callused palms along my hands. My forearms. My upper arms. And—and stops. Stops and just holds me against his body, not venturing to where I so loathe—so want—him to go.

"Relax, Devinee," he murmurs in my ear, his clean scent washing over me. "I can hear your heart racing."

I don't reply. I can no more stop my heart's gallop than I can pretend I'm not terrified of what's about to happen. That I'm not terrified of how much I *want* it to happen. "Just get it over with, Ellis." I tell him. "A deal is a deal. I'm here. Touch and be done with it."

I feel more than hear his sigh of frustration, but his voice is hard when he speaks.

"All right. As you wish." With one arm shifting to grip my waist and hold me in place, his free hand slides along my arm to my elbow. Strong callused fingers press into the flesh and joint from every angle imaginable, releasing the pressure just as tenderness turns to pain.

Confusion washes through me, prickling my skin. I know something is coming, and I want to skip to that part already. I don't need this foreplay. I don't want it. I want to get this over with.

Ellis moves my arm back and forth as if testing a hinge.

"You have an elbow fetish?" I ask through clenched teeth.

"Yes, very much so." He continues the motion a few more seconds before his hand slides to a new target: my bare torso.

I shiver, as much with the growing cold as with the light contact. My stomach clenches as his fingers slide across my skin, my heavy breasts tingling in anticipation of being touched. Despite myself, I can't help wondering what it will feel like to have this powerful male's hand slide over my breast, cupping its weight. Any moment now. Three. Two.

My nipples peak, poking harder through my flimsy bra, begging shamelessly for Ellis's fingers to tweak them. My breath stills.

But Ellis's hand skims over my ribs instead, tracing each one.

What the hell? I tilt back, looking at his face in question. But his eyes are intent on my body, examining it with a doctor's steady remove.

Changing course again, his touch returns toward my midline. Back to that breast he all but promised to fondle and never did. Closer. Closer still. And then he brushes *under* it, and under the strap of my bra, as if the tender orb was nothing but an obstacle. Reaching my sternum, he drops his perusal to the next rib down, the pressure firm and steady.

I jerk involuntarily, having somehow forgotten the huge-ass bruise blossoming along my side.

Ellis's hold on me tightens. In restraint. In comfort.

Lightening the pressure, he taps against the bone, watching my face intently.

I blink up at him, his broad shoulders and yellow eyes tightened with focus, and the pattern of his touch suddenly hits me. The male isn't fondling my breasts because he is busy retracing all the places his practice blade rapped this morning. Hell. He made his deal not to molest me, but to check whether I was all right. Because I would not let him check when he tried earlier.

"It's…sore." I whisper, surprising myself at the honesty.

Ellis nods, his face contrite instead of derisive. "I went too hard. I was angry." His jaw tightens. "I was jealous," he amends, his hand tightening into a fist that he slams against his thigh. "Bloody hell. You are mortal. I could have busted a rib. I'm glad I didn't." The last is said under his breath, his hand now openly moving among all the tender spots across my flesh without needing to search.

"Do you remember everywhere you struck?" I ask.

"Of course." Ellis sounds surprised at the question. "I know when I hurt you, Sam. I just don't let that stop me."

The sound of my first name on his lips sends a shiver through me. Something so simple made so intimate.

"It wasn't just my pride," I say, the words surprising myself as much as him. "When we were sparring. It wasn't just my pride keeping me from surrendering. It was… It was something else. I knew I couldn't make you stop, not if you didn't want to. And tapping to you just then, it—"

"It would have given me another weapon to use against you." Ellis finishes my sentence with all too much understanding. "And you didn't trust me not to do that." The statement carries no judgment.

I shiver suddenly, the cold autumn night roaring back in now that my mind doesn't swirl with confusion.

"Trust me, Sam," he murmurs, waiting for my nod before pulling his shirt over his head, the shifting muscles in his chest and shoulders even more overwhelming up close. When his arms tighten around me again, I slowly relax into his hold. His deliciously warm, velvet-skinned hold. Heat radiates off his body now that his sweat-soaked shirt is gone, and I can feel my own skin nearly purring in contentment as it warms back up.

For the next quarter hour, we settle into a comfortable silence, Ellis's cheekbone resting on the top of my head, the heat from his body seeping steadily into mine. I don't wonder at it. I don't question it after everything Ellis put me through. I just accept. I'm too tired and sore and scared to do anything else. With his heart so near my ear, I can feel and hear the *lub-dub, lub-dub* of his pulse. And I resist the fierce, crazy urge to shift my head until my lips press against it.

After a bit, his hand rubs gently over my ribs again, though this time, the touch is soothing instead of probing.

Too soothing. Too comfortable.

Finally, I jerk away from him, reality coming back to crash over me. This was a deal. And if he's decided he doesn't want to be sticking his cock into me just now, then I better take that and run. Especially given the very hard and very large bulge growing between his thighs.

Just because my body lusts after his just as badly as his seems to want mine doesn't mean I'm dumb enough to follow. "A deal is a deal, Ellis," I say. "Now, pay up."

He lets out a long sigh, the arms around me loosening to give me free rein to climb off his lap. "You'll find your answer on my chest," he says, shaking his head when I raise a brow. "That's the truth, Devinee. One you'd have seen already if you paid any attention. Left side, just over my first rib."

"Put your hands down to your sides," I instruct, half surprised when he obeys, the loss of his touch leaving me cold. A good reminder of reality. Twisting around to straddle his thighs, I lean down, looking for something—anything—in the dark, feeling the male tense under my inspection.

Now that I think about it, for all his muscled perfection, Ellis doesn't walk around without a shirt the way I'd expect a male like him to do.

My fingers join the search, smooth warm skin over taut muscle shifting under my touch. Ellis's ridged abdomen tightens, his breathing picking up slightly. Finally, not getting anywhere in the shadow, I take his huge shoulders and shift him firmly toward the moonlight—and gasp.

A star-shaped scar, about two inches across. Just like the one on Cassis's back. The same one a foster mother left on my palm. I open my hand to check, just in case.

"Did Sienna do this?" I ask, my fingers tracing the puckered flesh on Ellis's breast.

"Yes." Ellis flinches. "Cassis told you?"

"Only about himself. And when I asked what happened to her, Cassis said that what four immortals couldn't accomplish, the Spanish Inquisition took care of." I swallow, the thought of someone having cut into Ellis making my stomach turn. "That's why you sent me to Cassis, isn't it? You'd seen my mark, and you wanted to be sure I wasn't the same witch somehow. You knew Cassis would freak out and take a bite, learn the truth about me through my blood."

Ellis nods, his whole body tense as if bracing for a blow. He wants to discuss this topic as little as Cassis did, and yet…yet he put it on the table for our bargain.

My breath halts. "Why?" I ask. The intelligence in his eyes says he understands the question.

"Because the only way you'd let me touch you was if you thought I wanted something out of it."

"I don't understand what's happening," I whisper, my hand tight on Ellis's shoulder. "Why do I have the same mark as you and Cassis?"

"And Asher," Ellis says quietly. "Reese too. The four immortals who thought they could change the world and shattered themselves against it instead. The four horsemen."

"Weren't those supposed to bring about the end of the world?"

"They did," Ellis says softly. "The end of our world."

My heart squeezes at his words. Before I can think better of it, I flatten my palm over Ellis's chest, my scar covering his.

"No, Dev—" Ellis's panicked words cut off with a gasp as the marks…waken, pulling toward each other like magnets that guide each tiny groove into place. As a jolt of energy races through our joined bodies with the force of a lightning storm.

Power zaps through me.

One moment, I'm kneeling on Ellis's strong thighs, indulging in a curiosity. The next, the cold doesn't feel cold anymore, the woods blossoming into a rich bouquet of smells that separate each oak and fern and maple. Where a moment ago the forest's gentle shifting was a mere backdrop of white noise, now the whispering leaves and the rustle of a startled rabbit are as different as chords of music.

I swallow, my eyes focusing on Ellis's golden ones, my body knowing intuitively that it's his senses I'm looking through. And it's like putting on a pair of glasses after a lifetime of myopia. Except the shared sensations don't stop at the nice ones.

As I settle deeper into this strange shared bond, my heart pounding harder with each new sensation, a new feeling floods my veins. Pain. Burning pain encircling my wrists and ankles as if the metal bands touching my skin are made of hot coal. My breath catches, tears pressing against my throat, the shock nearly cutting off my air.

I feel as much as see Ellis's hand in motion, his intent clear. To break the connection, stop me from feeling his agony.

"Keep your hands where they are," I say, gritting my teeth, breathing through the pain. He opens his mouth to protest, eyes blazing, but I shake my head roughly.

Ellis lowers his hands obediently to his side, though I can feel the effort of will it takes him. His instinct screams at him to shield me from his pain. To protect his own soul from my scrutiny. But he fights it off. Because I asked.

"Why does it hurt so much?" I ask.

"Iron," Ellis says. "The same magic that makes me strong also makes me vulnerable."

I reach for his shackled wrist, and the male's arm shakes with the effort of keeping still while I trace the cuff, the angry red streaks snaking along his skin. When I touch the iron itself, I feel the phantom heat coming off it, burning away Ellis's magic bit by bit.

I hope iron doesn't hurt witches. Wrapping my fingers around each cuff, gripping all that searing heat, I pull it into myself. More and more, not knowing how I'm doing it, just knowing that I have to try. I pull every bit of fire into me until my nerves scream, until the feeling of a cool paste soothes the pain in Ellis's wrists.

"Devinee!" Ellis grips my arm, the red streaks now blistering my skin instead of his. "Stop."

I shake my head, my mind turning and fitting facts together like a game of Tetris. "I think it goes both ways, Ellis." I pant, watching my blistered skin settle into something calmer, my body fighting off the effects of iron more easily than Ellis's can. He looks dazed, his eyes wide on my smooth skin. "You share your strengths, and I share mine, even if my contribution is a simple tolerance to iron. We can do this. Survive. But we need a stronger connection."

Rising onto my knees, letting my screaming instincts lead, I press my mouth against his, my tongue brushing to part his lips.

Ellis gasps, his mouth opening to allow me inside, letting me explore his delicious heat for one stunned moment. And then he takes charge, surging off the cage bars into me. Gripping my face, he takes possession of my mouth with a power that echoes through every fiber of my body.

Our tongues tangle, magnifying our shared pain, yes—but magnifying our shared power even more. My sex clenches with the need for him, moving of its own accord in search of what it wants. I ride Ellis, grinding against his hard length until he pants with need.

Each stroke of his tongue sends a new rush of sensation through me, my thighs and feet and breasts all tensing. Tingling.

"Devinee," Ellis growls against me.

My free hand slides down his hard body, splaying over the ridges of his abdomen, teasing the waistband of his pants. His own fingers tangle in my hair, and he groans as the strength flowing through our connection overwhelms my soul.

Ellis

It took everything, every ounce of strength in every fiber of his being, for Ellis to pull his lips away from Sam's. Her hand was still on his heart, the connection between them filling him with a strength he'd not felt in centuries. Not since the witch Sienna had ripped him apart. Now, with Sam in his arms, Ellis wondered if perhaps the part of his soul he thought was dead had just been sleeping.

The pain in his wrists and ankles, where iron was slowly burning away his magic, had lessened beneath the cool balm of the witch's connection—even the red streaks of iron poisoning were now a gentle pink. Ellis didn't understand how the little witch had pulled the iron toward herself, but he knew for certain that he couldn't let her do it again. Not when he'd seen how it hurt her.

She was so small, so vulnerable, goose bumps breaking out on her skin as he pulled away from her, her dusky nipples hard under that threadbare white bra.

"Ellis," Sam whispered. The wind was ruffling the red streaks in her hair, her hazel eyes wide and glazed.

She wanted him. Her arousal had been there for a while, but Ellis could now smell the moisture slicking her thighs—though it was a wonder he could focus on anything over the painful pulsing in his cock. Gripping the bars of the cage on either side of him to keep from pouncing on her, Ellis took a ragged breath. He couldn't do this to her. Wouldn't risk what sex would do when a mere touch let her drag his poison toward herself.

"Move away," he whispered, flinching at the look of hurt that passed over Sam's eyes. "I want you, Devinee," he explained quickly. "I want you badly enough that I'm…I can barely hold myself back. But it isn't … I don't know what it's going to do to you. I'm not willing to risk it."

"So you get to decide for me?" Sam shot back, her forehead tensing with that spitfire spirit that made Ellis long to sheathe himself deep inside her in a single stroke. She stood suddenly, moving to the opposite-side cage bars. "What I should and shouldn't be risking. In what world is anything about my body your decision?"

Ellis laughed without humor. Oh, there were a lot of things about the witch's little body that he'd love to make decisions about. And despite Sam's words—which Ellis fully believed *she* believed— he could smell the excitement her body whispered to him at the mention of his control.

But with that connection of marks, that sharing of soul and pain, it scared Ellis as badly as anything he'd ever faced. What if Sam's desire was simply a mirror of his own? What if his overwhelming want was somehow coercing her?

More to the point, perhaps, was that Ellis was primal in a way Sam didn't understand. He didn't want to fondle and caress. He wanted to mate with every predatory wolfish instinct in his body, to take her. No reservations. The witch couldn't bear to have him on top of her in a sparring match, could not trust him to stop without savoring her surrender. If he were to allow himself free rein with her, it would require she trust him in a way he'd not yet earned. In a way she wasn't ready to give.

"Have you had sex before, Devinee?" Ellis asked, savoring the way the tips of her ears reddened at the bluntness.

"Yes." Her body tensed.

Ellis cocked his head. "By your own choice?"

She swallowed. "Yes."

Ellis's focus narrowed on the spike in her scent, the way her face paled with the answer. "You're lying." Rage filled him at the thought of the girl being forced. And the way he'd take her... Bloody hell.

"If you're so big on me making a choice, then maybe you should respect mine now," Sam shot back at him, her confidence faltering a moment later. "Unless you don't—"

"I *want* you," Ellis assured her with a frustrated chuckle. "But you deserve better, Samantha. Better than me." Rising and walking over to where she stood by the opposite cage bars, he crouched to keep from looming over her. "It won't be what you imagine. I won't —can't give you free rein over my body. I'll claim yours. Hard. And you..." He snorted softly. "I can already see you shaking at the thought."

Her eyes flared. "I'm shaking because I'm cold. Not because I'm afraid of you. I've never been afraid of you." The last part came out more softly. "The connection will make us stronger," she whispered. "Help us get out of here. I felt it happen with the kiss alone. I've had sex for pettier reasons than saving our lives."

Ellis nodded, the bravery in the little witch's eyes making his soul clench. He was a broken toy, and mating with Sam would be overwhelming for her while he took his fill. Oh, he could make her feel the pleasure, he would enjoy watching her scream in release as he brought her to climax over and over, but it would be on his terms. He was too much a predator, and she...

"Do it, Ellis," she whispered, hazel eyes burning with want. Conviction. "I can take—"

Ellis lunged at Sam, pinning her to the floor of the cage. Holding himself in a pushup position, he loomed over her small body, taking up all the space she considered hers. Inhaling the scent of her fear and thick pulsing desire.

"I can't make this gentle, Samantha." Ellis's words were ragged. "But I can stop now. I will always stop. But short of that... You'll have to trust me. Can you do that?"

A tremor ran through her, making those lush breasts tremble.

"I don't know." The truth of her words made her look even more vulnerable, more irresistible. Her mouth was open slightly, her full pink lips so inviting that Ellis wanted to suck on them as badly as he wanted to feel one of her nipples inside his mouth. Even now, the bunched peaks poked through her bra with the same insistence his cock pushed against his pants.

Shifting his weight onto one arm, he let his free hand roam the girl's body, watching her face as he finally cupped her breast, squeezed it—so full and tender that it must be aching—before brushing a thumb over her engorged nipple. The delicious sigh that escaped Sam's lips made his head spin.

He pressed his face into her flushed skin, inhaling deeply as he moved from her pulse down the length of her neck to her clavicle. Back up the other side. Growing dizzy on her spiked scent, making her breath come in small panting moans.

He spread his hand over her taut belly. She was small, but the muscles had been building in their time together, and her now-firm abdomen quivered beneath his touch. When he dropped his hand lower, edging into the top of her training pants, she shuddered and closed her eyes.

"No." His voice was harsh enough that her eyes snapped open, a gasp lifting her chest. Ellis glowered at her. "Keep your eyes on me. If you can't handle this, you won't be able to handle what comes next."

It came out sounding as much a promise as a threat, Sam's answering shiver of excitement and anxiety and arousal making Ellis forget the iron entirely. Holding her gaze, he untied the string at the top of her pants and slid his hand down until her moist panties greeted his fingers.

"Eyes on me," he said again. Sam's body trembled as he slipped under the waistline, over her silky hair, and brushed his thumb firmly between her folds. She moaned, nearly making him come right then. Wet and hot and as needy for him as he was for her. That was to say her *body* was ready. As for her mind... He brushed the top of her clit with the gentlest of pressures and poised his finger at her entrance, watching the witch tighten with anticipation. With anxiety.

Sam's wetness heated his fingers, and Ellis was certain she'd taste sweet with a bit of a spicy bite there, just as her mouth had. There was so much more of her to taste, to take under his power. If she would let him.

"Do you want me to stop?" Ellis asked, sounding strained, though he was ready to comply.

She shook her head.

"Tell me in words," he said. "Do you know that you can?"

"Yes," she breathed, the word hanging on her lips.

He held her gaze waiting—demanding—more.

"Yes, I know you will stop if I ask," Sam finished firmly, though Ellis could tell that it was her mind talking, her treacherous emotions still shifting with every breath. But that was all right. She would not learn the truth about her body and his until they started. "But I don't want you to stop."

"Brave witch." Leaning down on his arms, Ellis brushed a gentle kiss on Samantha's parted lips. A moment later, he thrust his finger inside her channel.

She clenched around him automatically, eyes glazed. She was so hot, so tight, her body constricting around the intrusion. Nervous even as she was needy.

He pumped his finger in and out several times, getting a feel for Sam's channel as she started to writhe beneath him. Pulling out, he ran his fingers all around her slick folds, teasing her apex until it hardened, swelling out of its hood. Until just the mere flick of his finger over her clit made her body arch beneath him.

Just as Sam started to gasp and buck, Ellis sat back on his heels and licked his fingers clean, letting the pleasure of her taste show in his face. Enjoying her wide, bewildered eyes. *Oh yes,* he thought at her as he sucked on his middle finger, *I like how you taste. I like it very much.*

And with that, he yanked Sam's pants and panties clean off.

29

Sam

Cool air brushes over my exposed skin, sending waves of ice and heat through my body. I'm exposed and naked, Ellis taking up all the space and air around me, my heart racing like a galloping horse as I'm on the ground, splayed before him. When I try to reach for him, he places a strong hand right on my sternum, pinning me to the ground, his knees pushing my thighs apart, his hands exploring my wet thighs.

The more I struggle against his hold, the more I discover how unyielding the male is, the power exuding from him as frightening as it is exciting. I've had sex before, for many reasons. To prevent a beating. To pay for debts I had no money to cover. I've had my body taken from me by force. But I've never been captivated like this, my sex longing for a man's touch. Totally out of control, able to do nothing but feel every magnified sensation.

Ellis's fingers makes their way possessively around my swollen clit, circling it on one side and the other as my hips buck beneath him. A moan escapes my lips, the emptiness inside me begging to be filled. I try to bring my thighs together to relieve the unbearable building pressure, stopping when Ellis's teeth snap wolfishly at the defiance.

Wrapping his arms around my thighs, the male yanks my bottom off the ground, and, before I can squeal in protest, strokes his tongue between my folds.

Fucking hell. I gasp, floundering against his unyielding hold. "Wait."

Ellis's yellow eyes grip me, pinning me in place. His white hair is loose around his face, jaw clenched. Demanding my trust. His cock, still in his pants, pulses against the fabric.

I take a deep breath and make my body settle. If Ellis is tasting me, he must be enjoying it. His cock certainly says he is. *Trust.*

With a small groan, he flicks my apex with the tip of his tongue, the sensation just enough to keep my arousal to a wild simmer without letting it leap to a full blaze. The wet *lap lap laps* fill my ears as the male returns his attention to my folds, each stroke sending a zing of sensation through me.

My toes curl, as the building need inside me rises and rises toward a great yawning abyss, my nails digging mercilessly into Ellis's shoulders.

I whimper, my need throbbing, the moisture between my legs growing thick and warm. Dripping. Heat rages through me, my hips undulating beneath Ellis's steel grip as his tongue laps up that slippery wetness.

"Ellis. Please." My voice is too desperate to be my own, but there's no surviving the blazing need that the male stokes with every *flick flick flick* of his tongue. "Please, damn you."

"No... I don't think so." His tongue draws a line through me. Lifting his face, the male licks drops of me from his lips. "I think I rather like seeing you this way."

His mouth descends on me again, this time circling mercilessly around my opening, which pulses in instant response. I gasp. Buck. Twist atop the rough ground of the cage in search of the release the warrior dangles before me.

"Please. Please. Please." The words spill, tripping over each other, the promise of coming pleasure so intense, it's too painful to bear.

The tip of Ellis's tongue traces my hood, brushing my engorged clit just enough to take my breath.

I moan, my head swimming, my body so deep in need that I'm dizzy with it.

"Now, Devinee," he growls, and for a moment, I don't understand the order until... Oh fuck. Sealing his mouth around my clit, Ellis *sucks*.

For a single moment, I try to fight it. To hold off the utter terrifying loss of control to free-falling pleasure. But I can't. Not with how far Ellis has pulled back the bowstring of my body's instinct before finally loosing me headfirst into release.

My thighs quiver as the first wave of the orgasm starts around my clit and spills like a storm along my nerves. Every muscle clenches, my nails leaving deep desperate marks along Ellis's shoulders. By the time the second and third waves come, I'm screaming into the night, my body and soul exposed and uncontrolled for Ellis to see.

My screams settle to low pants, my body feeling like a boneless mass void of strength. I didn't know it was like this—sex. The good kind. Maybe it usually isn't.

Ellis grips my hips. "I think you are ready," he says into my ear.

It takes me a moment to realize what he's talking about, and another moment to believe it. I can't do this again. Not *now*.

Except his hands are moving again, waking my tender sex. Stoking the fire with a skilled ease until I can't help writhing on the cage floor once more.

Sitting back, he frees himself from his pants, his cock springing out with so much force that a bead of moisture on the tip flies across the cage. Thick and erect, his cock twitches with each throbbing heartbeat, the velvety skin bulging from the pressure inside.

Just as I fully appreciate the sheer size of him, I realize there's no way he will fit inside me. Fit inside anyone. He can't.

"You can take me," Ellis says in a thick rasp as he flips me over onto my hands and knees. I'm about to protest, already looking back around at him, when I feel the heat of his hips hovering inches away from mine, feel his bulge pressing against my backside. Feel it slide through my wet folds, forward, back. Again. Then I can do nothing but press back against him mindlessly, a moan falling off my lips. With one hand, he reaches around to stroke my swollen clit, the traitorous little thing singing beneath his touch despite my trembling nerves.

Before I can brace myself, the great head slides easily through the slickness, filling my channel in one thrust. I cry out, the fullness and stretch and power so intense, I can't catch my breath. Then, with the next breath, the tightness from the penetration turns to the molten heat of pleasure as he strokes my clit with two callused fingers.

Ellis holds still inside me for a moment, letting me adjust to the great size of him, though truly, such a thing isn't possible. And then he starts moving. Slow, languid pumps that get faster and faster as I adjust, harder, our damp skin meeting loudly in the quiet night. His hips slam against mine in a rhythm that echoes through my whole body, his breaths growing harsh. I push back against him desperately, silently begging him to thrust deeper, panting into the darkness.

Wrong. It has to be wrong, this pleasure at the strength with which he holds me, giving no choice but to take him, no chance to move, to think.

Thrust thrust thrust.

Ellis's hot breath brushes the back of my neck, and a sharp sting pierces my shoulder.

"Mine." His growl is as primal as his bite, the claim vibrating through our connection. *Mine. Mine.* The meld of bite and claim penetrate deep into the darkness of my soul, which—for the first time ever—yawns open wide in answer, just as Ellis's seed fills me, our joint cries of release carrying to the stars.

Yes, yes, yes, my soul agrees over the waves of orgasm contorting my body. *Finally. I've been waiting.*

Fucking hell. My damn soul talks.

3 0

Ellis

*E*llis couldn't tear his eyes away from Sam's delicious body, the scent of sex and pleasure clinging to her like perfume. His scent clinging to her. She was gorgeous when she climaxed, a pink flush rising to her skin and face, her body quivering. Bloody hell, she was gorgeous all the time.

He swallowed as she pulled on her clothes, the pants sliding over the full curve of her hip, her rebellious red hair flipping in the wind as if it were embodying the same wild spirit that the little sprite contained. It made him hard all over again.

Though he tried not to make it obvious, he couldn't stop tracking her, drinking in her every small motion while his soul repeated the word he'd screamed as he'd taken her. The word he hoped she wouldn't remember as much as he hoped she would. *Mine.*

Samantha Devinee was his. His mate, though fae rarely had such things nowadays—though he hadn't found one in the hundreds of years he'd been alive and had never expected to.

Bloody hell.

Ellis hadn't understood the full meaning of mating until after it happened, when he'd been inside Sam and felt a missing piece of his soul find itself deep in hers.

His jaw tightened, and he shimmied himself into his pants.

The problem was that his soul hadn't been just unfulfilled before —it'd been broken. Or, more accurately, had a piece broken off. And his gut told him Sienna might have been behind that.

Mating within a species was rare. Between species?—Unheard of. Which strengthened Ellis's suspicion that this was orchestrated. It had to be. Crazy as it sounded, he was sure that Sienna had somehow carved out a slice of all their souls and set them waiting. Waiting for a witch who would not be born for centuries, but who would one day carry those shards inside her. Connecting the species together—finally completing the work the horsemen had set out to do all those years ago, when the world was not yet ready for it.

That would certainly explain how broken Sienna had left the four of them. How perfectly Sam had filled his jagged wound.

Ellis's heart sank, the darkness that Sam had lifted descending on him once again. She couldn't know. He couldn't tell her. She deserved to have her own life, make her own choices, find her own love—not play out a role assigned to her by a sadistic dead witch. Ellis might be a slave to Sienna's machinations, but he would ensure that Sam, at least, would be free.

"Ellis?"

He paused, hands on the shirt he was about to pull over his head. Poised on her knees, Sam cradled her marked palm, her face tight.

"What is it?" Ellis crouched beside her, his heart spurred into a gallop. She'd buffered the iron's effect on his magic, but was it hurting her now? Bloody hell. He gripped her wrist. "What's wrong?"

She blinked up at him, plainly confused by the overreaction, and Ellis schooled his face quickly. This would be another new thing to get used to now that Ellis's mating bond had snapped into place, his instinct to protect her at all costs. "What's wrong, Devinee?" he repeated, finally managing to summon up the proper distance for his voice, as if nothing of importance had happened between them.

Sam flinched away as if struck, a rare wave of vulnerability fluttering over her face before she pulled herself together. It tore at him, hurting her. But it was better this way. For her, if not him. Cocking a brow, Ellis waited for the answer.

"I'm not sure," she said, her heartbreaking soprano clear and distant.

"Then I'm not sure I can help." He started to rise. "Let me know when you find words."

Yes. He was an arse.

"My blood's vibrating," Sam snapped, stopping him in midmotion. "It feels like there's a swarm of bees buzzing inside my blood. Do you know what that is or not?"

"A buzzing," Ellis repeated, her words now gripping all his attention. "Inside your blood. Like liquid power?"

"Yes... Yes. That sounds right." Sam's brows pulled together, her too-intelligent eyes boring into him. "You know what it is." Not a question this time.

Ellis scrubbed a hand over his face. Their mating had unlocked the witch's magic. Lovely.

3 1

Sam

I shift my weight, staring suspiciously at Ellis. The damn male is as volatile as a teenage girl. My fault for having started to care. For believing those words he growled when he was inside me. *Mine.*

"Earth to bloody Ellis. Will you tell me what's going on with me or not?" I step closer to him, intending to shake his shoulder, but the proximity agitates that swarm of phantom bees to new levels. With Ellis's bare, marked chest just inches away, my hand moves of its own accord, like the compulsion of a vampire but a million times stronger.

Ellis knows something. My body whispers to me. *And I need to know it too.*

Without thinking or stopping, I give in, laying my hand over the male's chest. This time, the rush of power flowing through me feels more like a volcanic eruption than a yellowjacket outing.

My body shakes, and I'm aware in a peripheral way that Ellis is calling my name, the words, "Devinee? Devinee," echoing through the forest without meaning.

I'm plunged into darkness. A tunnel, like a slide at a playground, except this one opens to a sea of terror.

I'm shackled. No, not me. I know it's Ellis's eyes I'm looking through, his hands that are shackled with iron chains. We are in a small, dim room, with three males. With a woman who is a witch.

"Devinee."

A scream pierces the air, echoing off the damp stone walls, the voice familiar. When I turn my head, I find Cassis strapped to a splintery work table, howling in pain as the witch carves his back with a wooden stake. Asher and Reese struggle against their binds.

The hatred filling my blood is enough to make me howl to the moon, the promise of vengeance echoing in my blood.

"Devinee!" The voice calling me now turns from worry to sheer command. "Devinee, get out of my head. Now!"

I obey, gripping on to the voice's strength to drag myself from the historic dungeon into the fresh, cool forest of the now. My mouth is dry, my mind working through what I just saw. Through the fact that while my mind has escaped the darkness of Ellis's memories, the power buzzing inside my veins is still there.

Ellis pulls my hand away from his chest, and, from the ache in my wrist, I realize he's been trying to wrench it away for some time.

"What… How?"

Ellis's face is hard. "Magic. That's the liquid power you were feeling. The one I was starting to tell you about when you decided to take a trip down my memory lane. It's the same magic that's responsible for this." Lifting his shackled wrist, he shows me his corded forearm, the smooth skin showing no sign of iron poisoning.

Magic. Inside me. No fucking way.

"Do you still feel the power?" Ellis asks, his gaze intent on my face.

I swallow, too many questions filling my mind to form a meaningful sentence just yet. "Tell me more about Sienna," I ask instead, pivoting the conversation. "Why did she torture you?"

Ellis's lips tighten, the lines in his chiseled face growing deeper. "I don't know, Devinee. I'm not a witch. You're the one who launched herself into my mind. You tell me."

I recoil, though I should be used to his blows by now. Then again, he's right. I had no right to connect the marks, to intrude into the male's senses and memories without permission. Even if I didn't know exactly how the connection worked.

"I'm sorry."

The male sighs, shaking himself. "It was in the middle of the fae-vamp wars," he says. "Asher and I, both royal bastards, had gotten it into our heads to make peace between the races instead. Cassis and Reese were of the same mind. Call us a rebel force, if you will. To top it off, Cassis was in love with a witch. Sienna, who said she had an idea that might help our cause. We trusted Cassis, and so we agreed to trust her enough to meet."

Ellis bristles. "It was a different time, Devinee. A time when being female meant you were assumed to be weak. Meek. And that's what Sienna acted like—and the four idiots that we were, we never questioned it. Then she'd convinced Cassis to gather us all in her lair. That's when she struck."

"How long did she keep you there?" I shudder, wondering how Ellis could ever look a witch in the face after what I saw there.

"A decade." His face closes off again, as if that is the most he's going to say on the subject. "Then she was killed in the Inquisition, just like all the others. Until you, frankly, I thought we were rid your kind. And until you," he adds more quietly, "I thought that was for the best."

I bite my lip, though he tries to take the sting out of the words by brushing a thumb across my cheek. It can't. Nothing can take the sting out of the truth, as I well know from the darkness that keeps washing over me.

"Devinee," Ellis snaps, his hold on my chin tightening until I'm forced to look at his yellow eyes and nothing more. "What you saw in me, it happened centuries ago. Pull your mind the hell out of there and don't go back. Ever. Understand?"

"Of course," I say, hoping he'll believe the lie. Because there's no way I can ever unknow how a witch hurt him and the others.

Forcing a smile to my face, I swing my attention back to the buzzing inside my blood. "So there's magic inside me now? Do you think it'll stay?"

"You're a witch," Ellis says bluntly. "The magic was always there. Now that you can access it, however, an opening spell would be helpful." He shakes the door of the cage in emphasis, one eyebrow raised.

"Yeah. Unfortunately, this newfound magic came without an instruction manual."

"Then it's a good thing I spent a decade chained inside a witch's dungeon," says Ellis, settling me onto the ground beside him. "I'll show you what the tracing looks like, and you can try it on the lock."

"How do you know I won't need an eye of newt or toe of frog or something?" I ask, lifting my brow as the male traces something that looks like an Egyptian rune on the dirt floor.

"Do you have a better idea?"

"Fair point." Kneeling on the ground, I use my nail to copy his drawing—which turns out to be a great deal more complicated than I expected. I don't get it right. Not the first time. Or the fifth. On the fifteenth time, however, as I make the final squiggle thing on the edge, I feel the rune call to the magic inside me. A moment later, the very earth beneath Ellis and me cracks open with a booming scrape of rock and tearing roots.

I yelp.

The cage rocks.

The earthy maw yawns and settles at about a foot wide, the whole cage now tipping while Ellis and I grab on to each other for balance.

"Bloody hell," the male mutters. "Well, we know it works. Now try it on the lock."

Taking the padlock, I have him sketch the rune on the ground again while I use a bit of mud to copy it onto the metal. The buzzing of magic inside my blood condenses into a single swarm, and I feel it fill the rune, the metal vibrating against the bars.

Grabbing me from behind, Ellis throws me to the other side of the cage, his body covering mine as the lock explodes into dozens of shards, some of them flying past my face. When he lets me up, the back of his shirt bloody, I can see his body trembling no matter how hard he tries to hide it.

"How badly are you hurt?" I ask.

Ellis shrugs a muscular shoulder in a *don't know, don't care* gesture that I believe. But if it isn't the wounds from the explosion that are making beads of sweat appear on his brow, then…

"What did Sienna use the opening spell for?" I ask, making his gold eyes meet mine.

"Isn't the name self-explanatory?"

"No." My fingers curl. "You made it sound like a harmless little thing, but it isn't harmless at all, is it? And not just because it worked too well."

"I had no choice," Ellis says unapologetically. "In case you haven't noticed, we're sitting ducks here. You needed to feel confident to have a chance of this working, and I gave you what you needed. Now, let's get the hell out of here."

I grab his wrist, his breathing only now settling. "Tell me what Sienna used the spell for."

"To open us," he says, holding open the cage door for me.

3 2

────────

Sam

*E*llis is silent and lethal as he leads me back to the Academy, the darkness giving him little pause. As we approach the edge of the wood, he tells me to go directly to the barrack while he drags Asher out of bed to deal with everything.

"Devinee." Grabbing my shoulder before I walk off, he levels me with a stern glare. "You stay put. Don't talk to anyone. Don't go anywhere. Don't even leave your bloody room for drill until I come and get you. Clear?"

I wasn't planning to, but I flip Ellis off anyway before heading to my room. The little snarl he sends my way makes me smile.

The barrack is quiet and dark as I slip inside, the cadets all sleeping off the day. Despite my rude gesture to Ellis, my pulse is fast and shallow as I quickly jog up to my room, the memories of what happened earlier chasing my steps. With distance from Ellis, the power inside me calms, buzzing bees settling to sleep. It's as much a comfort as a fright.

My nerves calm a bit at the sight of my door, and I wonder whether my willingness—my *want*—to hide in my room makes me a

195

coward. I push the thought away. It doesn't matter, because I wasn't planning on being a hero to begin with. Between Bernadette's attacking me and Quinn doubling down on the plan by adding a touch of murder and captivity to the recipe, I'm more than happy to leave the mess to Ellis to handle.

Ellis. The male's image comes unbidden to my mind, sending a flare through my nerves. The man is too powerfully beautiful for his own good—and for mine. We had sex. Great, mind-blowing, thigh-slicking sex—the first I've ever had. But that was it. Being trapped in close quarters leads to all sorts of stupidity, and from the way he pulled away from me once the final aftershocks ended, he was already over the coupling. Just because it was my first not-terrible fuck doesn't make it anything but a fuck. Not to a guy. Not to an immortal male who's probably had more females than a rabbit.

Shoving Ellis from my mind, I open the door to my room and savor the familiar sight. My dresser stands half-open, the bed just as unkempt and blanketless as I left it when I ran out. No Bernadette. Her murder hits me anew suddenly, seeming so long ago now. Her multicolor scrunchies sit in a bowl on the corner of her desk, one workout tee slung over the back of her chair. She may have tried to kidnap and murder me, but still, somehow, this isn't what I would have wished for her.

Taking a piece of wood I whittled into a doorstop a few days ago, I jam it beneath my door, testing it for security. The doorstop holds. My breath eases with that, though I still stay away from the window and keep the lights turned off. I don't know who I think I'm hiding from, but at least I'm doing something.

Setting course for the darkest corner of the room—old habits die hard—I—

A hard hand clamps around my mouth, the dark shadow having moved faster than I thought possible. The cold laughter in my ear sends my pulse into an outright gallop as the scent of rotting meat makes my stomach roil.

Quinn. Quinn here in my room. Waiting for me in the dark.

"So, the witch does have power." His words are honey soft in my ear. "I thought so. When something that should be there doesn't manifest, add stress. Enough stress, enough motivations, and voilà. A working witch. Here, come take a look at something."

Switching his grip on my mouth to the other hand, Quinn pulls a cell phone out of his pocket and taps the screen to show a night-vision-green version of the cage I was in. No sound comes from the device, but the swaying leaves prove that the feed is live, though the battery power in the camera is running low. A tiny slap-on the bastard must have stuck on a tree branch before leaving.

My chest tightens so hard, I can barely draw breath. A setup. The whole thing was a setup.

"Ellis will kill you," I hiss to Quinn.

The vampire laughs. "Ellis, harm me over a witch? You really know nothing about him. He'll thank me for cleaning up for him— you were a fuck. Nothing more. Or did you not see how quickly he dropped you once his cock softened?"

My heart twitches because Ellis *did* pull away, his face hardening as some invisible wall slammed between us.

"I can replay that part of the video for you if you'd like," Quinn offers. "Just in case you had doubts. He came for you because that's his punishment, the reason he got sent to Talonswood. But he sure as hell isn't going to do anything but celebrate once you're out of his hair."

Not true. At least not all of it. *But some is, isn't it?*

I make myself snort with indifference. "Have you met Ellis? Does he seem like the kind of male who'd let you put him in iron without retribution?"

"I'm Count Victor's son, and Ellis is the Talon king's bastard. If you think a bit of jest is the worst we've done to each other over the centuries, you are even more gullible than I imagined. Now then—"

I elbow him with all my might, my bone connecting with solid, unmoving muscle.

Quinn's grip on the back of my neck tightens painfully, his tone changing to an anger-fueled growl. "Don't get stupid, witch. Not when I can snap your neck by accident." He shakes me like a kitten, my bones rattling.

"What do you want?"

"You," he answers. "The first witch in so long with the magic flowing in her blood. It had to be there. It was just a matter of unlocking it. And now, I'm going to deliver you to the count—just as soon as I sample the goods."

Shoving me forward, Quinn throws me onto my bed, my shins hitting the sideboard. Panic rushes over me, and I twist, kicking at him as hard as I can. I try digging up the buzzing bees inside my blood—only to find the power gone. Just like Ellis.

Quinn's eyes gleam as he approaches, his tongue flicking over his lips as his pants bulge. The dark widow's peak against his pale skin makes the vampire look like the monster he is.

I shove myself up, scrambling to get off the bed—the back of my mind noting that Quinn must have a reason for letting me move at all. That he's just playing with his food.

I'm right. Just as my muscles flex for the final shove, the vampire is on top of me, his hand gripping my neck, pinning me back to the crumpled sheets while the bed sags beneath his added weight. Leaning his face toward mine, Quinn licks my cheek and comes up grinning.

"Fear. One of my favorite flavors." With his free hand, he grips one of my breasts and squeezes painfully. "Pain is my second favorite, if you were wondering."

Don't feel. Don't feel. Don't feel.

I draw a breath past my constricted airway, focusing on each lungful of air. I can't fight the vamp off, not right now. But I might still get an opportunity. I'll make an opportunity.

"Do you know why you're not screaming?" Quinn asks, his words a painful mockery of my thoughts. "Because you're smarter than you look. You know no one will come, don't you? Of course you do. Your own roommate was ready to serve your head up on a platter—what do you imagine the rest of the delinquents here would do if they discovered you helpless?"

I swallow, and Quinn's smile deepens. "That's right. They'll be getting popcorn. Or come to the door in hopes of collecting whatever scraps I leave. No one ends up in Talonswood for being an upstanding citizen. Why don't you try it for yourself, Samantha? Scream. Beg."

His grip on my breast tightens, and it's all I can do to bite back the howl of pain I can tell the bastard is seeking.

Quinn's nostrils flare. "Beg!"

3 3

———————

Sam

Beg. Surrender. Yield.

My heart pounds, my breaths quick and shallow. Blood rushes through my body so quickly that my vision narrows, my muscles tight and ready—with nowhere to go.

I've been here before. Have met so many Quinns. Immortality is not so different from humanity when it comes to power.

"This is how quickly a vampire is going to take you down, Devinee." Ellis's phantom words hiss through my memories, the bed beneath feeling rough as sand. *"He is going to take you down and rip into your jugular, and then he's going to drink all the blood pouring through that little, fragile body of yours. Now, tap out and get the hell off my pitch like you wanted."*

Like I wanted. A shudder runs through me. Like *I* wanted. Ellis is an arrogant ass. A hard-as-nails ass who gave me no mercy on the pitch but knew exactly where each of his strikes landed. Who offered me his pain as collateral, because I would not trust him otherwise.

Quinn is wrong. Ellis might not like me, but if I call him, he will come. Somehow, after everything, I trust him enough to know that.

201

My hand curls into a fist, the brand on my palm tingling as I concentrate my thoughts on the male who's been inside me. Who can help me now. Who can hurt me more deeply than anything Quinn could ever do.

My heart pauses, frozen in a sudden rush of fear that has nothing to do with the vamp on top of me. Shoving though it, I holler anyway. "Ellis!"

Quinn slaps me across the mouth, blood spattering onto my tongue. "Your fuck buddy is not even in the building."

"Ellis," I shout again, using all the air in my lungs. My call bounces off the stone walls, the closed window. Echoing and repeating itself. My mark tingles again, my need for Ellis waking the liquid power inside my blood. The primal raw truth beneath the call makes the air inside the room move. "Ellis, *help*!"

The air swirls as if trying to carry my words outside, the small phantom breeze picking up with each heartbeat. More and more. My hair ruffles, Quinn's eyes widening in confusion as a gust of wind strikes his face and continues moving. Swirling. Crashing into the window, and again harder, shattering it to bits, just like his damned phone.

Quinn shoves away from me, twisting into a fighter's crouch toward the small explosion.

Inside the room, the wind picks up even more as I feel Ellis's answering call tugging on the bond inside me. The male heard me. Is coming. Is close. I don't know how I know, but I do.

The swirling air turns into a small cyclone that clips the edge of my writing desk, breaking the wood.

Holy hell.

I dash for the door. Yank on it, hitting the very doorstop I pushed into place.

"I'll kill you, bitch," Quinn growls, his sharp canines on full display as he grabs my hair and uses it to slam me into my dresser.

Pain rakes though my body. The storm picks up with it. Outside, voices are starting to shout, the broken window apparently having gotten attention. Someone bangs on the closed door. The handle rattles. The noises meld together as the pain and magic flare, the strength I felt in the cage with Ellis filling me once again. Raising my arm, I shove at Quinn with everything I have.

And a wall of air throws the vampire across the room.

"Devinee," Ellis shouts from the hallway. "Open the door! It's me."

I glance over my shoulder toward the door, but don't move. Now that I have Quinn pinned against the wall, I don't dare let go. The air cocooning him is moving so fast that it presses into his neck, cutting off his breath. I wonder how much air vampires actually need, whether Quinn can survive long without breathing. I wonder whether I care.

Grabbing one of the wooden splinters from my shattered writing desk, I advance on the vamp. Darkness fills me. Darkness and cold and pain. My heart calms, my eyes narrowing on the vampire's chest. My hand tightens around the makeshift stake.

The door crashes open behind me, magic coursing through me stronger still as Ellis steps into the room. From the corner of my eye, I see him hold his forearm against the storm as he forges his way toward Quinn and me.

"Don't, Devinee," Ellis shouts. "The arse will answer for what he did, but you aren't a killer."

"You're the one who was working on making me one, weren't you?" The anger and darkness inside me spiral upward in concert with my growing power. I flick my hand, and the torrent of air stops, the solid oak of Bernadette's headboard suddenly sprouting branches that pin Quinn's wrists and ankles. Just as Quinn would have held me down. The way the rapists in the foster system grabbed only little skinny wrists, because the children—because I— had no power.

Guess what, asshole? This pup grew up.

The vampire screams, arching against the restraint. For a moment, I'm certain that his muscled body will rip through my hold, but it doesn't. No. This time, it's me who has the upper hand.

"Stop," Quinn screams as I take a step toward him, my stake aiming for his heart. His dark eyes are wide, the dilated pupils speaking of a sad attempt at compulsion.

I shake my head. Quinn didn't stop, did he? Not when he attacked me. Not when he murdered Bernadette. None of the other Quinns of the world stopped either. I draw my hand back and—

Strong hands grab me from behind, and I inhale a familiar male musk as Ellis shoves me away from Quinn. Before I can recover, Ellis pulls a wicked-looking blade from his boot and, in a single violent motion, slices it across Quinn's throat. Blood spills onto the vampire's chest, pulsing with a rare occasional beat of his heart as it slowly drains away, every last drop.

Numbness settles over me, the dead vampire's sightless eyes filling my vision. Dead. Quinn is dead. Ellis killed him. The oak vines holding Quinn's body in place die as well, the magic inside me flickering in too many directions to do much of anything.

Dropping the knife, Ellis wraps his arms around me and turns me away from the scene. My face presses into his clean shirt, his wild fresh scent filling my lungs as the steady beat of his heart grounds me in reality. The horror of what almost happened to me, of what I almost did, of what Ellis *did* do.

"Why did you…" I bury my face in Ellis's shoulder, my whole body shaking as the male holds me tight—the male who answered my call, who came to help. To save me. Not from Quinn, as it turns out, but from myself. "You said I wasn't a killer, but you…"

"Because I am what you are not," Ellis whispers into my hair, his callused hand rubbing a soothing circle between my shoulder blades. "Don't ever become me, Sam."

34

Sam

Ellis gives my shoulder a squeeze before releasing me as a horde of people rush into the room. Asher, Reese, the Academy guards with blades drawn.

Raising his palms in proof that no resistance will be offered, Ellis steps toward them and lowers to his knees. At Asher's nod, one of the guards retrieves Ellis's bloodied knife, two more twisting the male's hands behind his back. The snap of handcuffs around his wrists is deafeningly loud.

Loud enough to restart the breath I hadn't realized I was holding. "Wait!" I step forward, Reese's hard arm blocks my path. "Wait. He was protecting me. Quinn was going to—"

"Quinn does not seem to have been capable of doing much of anything," Asher snaps, jerking his chin toward where the dying oak vines are still holding the dead vampire in place. Throwing Quinn's corpse a look of undistilled hatred, Asher orders the guards to take Ellis to lockup.

My heart pounds.

"Asher!" My words hit the fae male's broad uniformed back, his mussed hair.

Grabbing the top of my arm, Reese yanks me in the opposite direction.

THREE HOURS LATER, I'm sitting in a sterile infirmary room, the stern medic who examined and sutured me having tossed me a set of scrubs to change into before leaving. That was two hours ago, and the locked door has not opened since. Hearing a key scrape the lock now, I get anxiously to my feet.

Stepping inside, Reese runs his eyes over me, his expression cold. "No life-threatening injuries," he says, reading from a clipboard in his hand, his tall, lithe body turning even that routine motion into a dance. "A mild concussion. You are released."

"What's happening to Ellis?" I ask, my pulse speeding anew.

"He'll be bleeding a great deal more than you are," Reese says evenly, his starkly handsome face and flat blue eyes giving nothing away. "That's as far as I can promise you. Beyond that, it will be up to Count Victor. I don't imagine anyone from the Council will step in, given it was the count's own offspring who Ellis murdered."

"Reese." Before I can think better of it, I cover the two paces of space between us and grab his wrist, the cool muscles jumping under my fingers as if trying to get away from my touch. A muscle in his hard jaw tics as he looks down at me. "None of this is Ellis's fault. It's mine. Well, it's Quinn's and Bernadette's, but if you need to blame someone who's still alive, then blame me."

Reese yanks his arm from my grasp with a crisp, deliberate chop. "We are not on a first-name basis, Ms. Devinee." The coolness of his body matches his tone. "As for who is at fault for what, there's plenty to go around. Follow me."

Saying nothing more, the male leads me across the green to the administrative building, the sign *Dean's Office* flashing before me as we enter. Asher, Ellis—his hands still shackled behind his back—and Victor are already inside, the count sitting behind a grand mahogany desk with an open laptop before him. Tall windows line the wall behind him, letting in the first rays of misty dawn light.

"…reportedly, the girl had an absurd notion that I would be attracted to a cadet trapped in a cage," Victor is saying to someone on the screen. "Whatever gave her that idiotic idea remains unknown. However, I can confirm that the body of Bernadette Yalls, demivampire, was found in the woods. Cause of death is consistent with neck trauma." He glances up at me. "You saw Quinn snap the girl's neck?"

I blink, forcing myself to sound as firm and reasonable as Victor. "Errr. Yes, sir. I did. He——"

Victor's attention is already back on his screen, an unfamiliar voice sounding from the speakers.

"Is there evidence of an assault on the witch?"

My face heats.

"She claims Quinn attempted sexual assault but did not succeed. However, several other cadets have come forward claiming the male has done as much to them."

Silence fills the room, the people on the other end of the video conference seeming to have muted their mikes in deliberation. Taking advantage of the lull, I try to make eye contact with Ellis, but he never deviates from the alert pose he holds. Beside him, Asher is scowling as he watches the ongoing conference call—though from what I can tell so far, Count Victor is actually a voice of bloody reason.

"Count Victor." The computer speaks again, while the count taps his finger on the tabletop. "Given your relationship to Quinn… the Council is ready to hear your recommendations. It is our hope that the situation can be resolved to everyone's satisfaction. We would, of course, consult with King Bryant before a drastic measure against Ellis is taken, but given——"

"That will not be necessary." Victor flicks his hand dismissively, both Asher's and Ellis's brows drawing together in quickly hidden surprise. "Our good king of Talon has been using his bastard to do his dirty work for the past four centuries and will do little but celebrate the death of one more vampire. I think it best if I manage the situation myself. Someone certainly needs to be handling this mess."

"What exactly are you implying, Victor?" a new voice pipes up from the computer.

"Exactly what you heard, Dean Javin. That when it comes to running a reform school, you are no more useful than a doormat. I'd have thought the four assaults and two murders that happened on your lack of watch would speak for themselves, but perhaps not." Victor's tone hardens. "When Talonswood Reform was created, we all acknowledged that we were dealing with delinquents. That this place had to be run with an iron hand, which *Dean* Javin has either forgotten or overlooked."

Victor shakes his head at the screen. "It is the responsibility of the Talonswood administration to create an environment where illegal behavior isn't simply not tolerated, but is not given an opportunity to happen in the first place. A responsibility Javin has shirked. As such, given that I am already here, I call for an immediate Council vote to have Talonswood placed under my command."

The ringing silence of muted mikes fills the air again, then four high-pitched rings and one low buzz sound from the speakers, making the corner of Victor's mouth twitch in pleased acknowledgment. "I will report my progress shortly," he tells the people on the screen before closing his laptop and surveying the room with an ice-cold gaze.

"Playtime is over, Mr. Asher." Victor's words send a chill down my spine. "Welcome to the new Talonswood Reform."

THE ADVENTURE CONTINUES in LAST CHANCE REFORM, Immortals of Talonswood Book 2. If you are reading an ebook version of this book, please continue for a FREE preview of Alex Lidell's best-selling reverse harem fantasy romance, POWER OF FIVE.

TILDOR

THE CADET OF TILDOR

ABOUT THE AUTHOR

Alex Lidell is an Amazon KU All Star Top 50 Author Awards winner (July, 2018). Her debut novel, THE CADET OF TILDOR (Penguin, 2013) was an Amazon Breakout Novel Awards finalist. Her Reverse Harem romances, POWER OF FIVE and MISTAKE OF MAGIC, both received Amazon KU Top 100 awards for individual titles.

Alex is an avid horseback rider, a (bad) hockey player, and an ice-cream addict. Born in Russia, Alex learned English in elementary school, where a thoughtful librarian placed a copy of Tamora Pierce's ALANNA in Alex's hands. In addition to becoming the first English book Alex read for fun, ALANNA started Alex's life long love for fantasy books. Alex lives in Washington, DC.

Join Alex's newsletter for news, special offers and sneak peeks: https://links.alexlidell.com/News

Find out more on Alex's website: www.alexlidell.com

SIGN UP FOR NEWS AND RELEASE NOTIFICATIONS

Connect with Alex!
www.alexlidell.com
alex@alexlidell.com

9 781949 347142